WIDOWS OF BLESSINGS VALLEY:

Elizabeth

MAXINE DOUGLAS

Widows of Blessings Valley: Elizabeth
by Maxine Douglas

ABOUT THE BOOK

Late morning mining accident casts a gloom over the town of Blessings Valley. Over twenty souls were lost in an excavating explosion that has left several widows, friends, and townspeople mourning. The explosion occurred as the miners were coming out for lunch. A rescue force was sent out immediately to recover the bodies. Services are currently being arranged. Pray for these lost souls and their families.
—*Blessings Valley Chronicle*

Elizabeth Hamilton is a mess – her husband was killed in a mining accident, and she's been left nearly penniless as she struggles through the grief and betrayal to her husband's memory.

Augustine Raines believes there is no woman who will truly love him after a freak riding accident has left him scarred, and that his only attraction is a healthy bank account.

NOTE FROM THE AUTHOR

Elizabeth is the first in the *Widows of Blessings Valley* series. While it is always a thrill for an author to start a new series, it was with a heavy heart that I was compelled to write this one. I became a widow in April 2018 after a brief battle with cancer took my love from me to be with our Lord. During those agonizing first few months, so many questions flitted into my mind, along with the anger, grief, loneliness, and finally, acceptance that my beloved was really gone from this realm. It was some of those questions that inspired this series. I hope that it will let other widows, and widowers, know that they are not alone with the crazy questions that come to mind. That as they wonder what is or isn't appropriate—should they remove their ring(s), when, if at all, should they start dating, are they still married or now considered single, what is the proper mourning period in our modern times, when will the anger go away, and the list goes on and on—others are experiencing similar emotions and questions. While I don't expect this series to be the answer to the grieving of the reader, I do hope that I have somehow eased that feeling of being alone...for you are not.

Here start the stories of Elizabeth, Vera, Stella, Fannie, Vivian, Charlotte, Violet, and Willa herself—they are the *Widows of Blessings Valley.*

ACKNOWLEDGEMENT

Thank you to Pastor David Thompson of the First Lutheran Church in Chickasha, Oklahoma, for his assistance in helping me choose the bible passages for this series.

The church and the congregation have become my extended family.

I'd be lost spiritually without all of you.

DEDICATION

To all those who have grieved the passing of a
loved one.
To my friends Callie and Maria who supported and
encouraged me during the writing of this first book
in this series after the loss of my husband.
To Carla who is always willing to read for me at a
moment's notice.
Without all of you this book may never have been
written.

In loving memory of my soulmate, the love I waited
a lifetime for.
We'll find each other again~we always do.

A TIME FOR EVERYTHING

"For everything there is a season, and a time for
every matter under heaven;
a time to weep, and a time to laugh;
a time to mourn, and a time to dance;"
Ecclesiastes 3:1, 4

PROLOGUE

Late morning mining accident casts a gloom over the town of Blessings Valley. Over twenty souls were lost in an excavating explosion that has left several widows, friends, and townspeople mourning. The explosion occurred as the miners were coming out for lunch. A rescue force was sent out immediately to recover the bodies. Services are currently being arranged. Pray for these lost souls and their families.

—Blessings Valley Chronicle

On a gray, chilling morning in the spring of 1892, seven women, all dressed in black, widows before their time, mourn with the people of Blessings Valley as the preacher begins the funerals of their husbands lost in a coal mining explosion. Sorrow etched on each of the ashen faces. All hope gone from their eyes.

Wilhelmina Alexander knows firsthand those feelings creeping into their minds and hearts. The anger. The grief. The questions of what to do next. The wondering of how they will ever survive. The betrayal if they ever find love again.

As the preacher concludes the last of his sermon, Willa promises those seven souls she'll look after their wives. Help them learn to live again.

CHAPTER 1

Early Summer 1892

Elizabeth Hamilton stood in the middle of her small living room, twisting the wedding band on her left ring finger. She sucked in her bottom lip, hoping to stop the pain that never ceased to overwhelm her.

This had been their home—her and Steven's. The place where they'd made plans to one day raise a family.

That dream was gone.

Steven was gone.

She wrapped her arms tightly around her trembling body. The suppressed anger in her from the past several months had reached its boiling point. The tears she'd fought so hard to hold back burst forth like a raging river after a storm.

With an agonized scream, she clenched her hands tightly into fists and dropped to her knees. "You promised, Steven Hamilton! You promised to never leave me. You promised we'd be together forever. You promised, you promised, damn you, you promised…" Elizabeth's body gave in to the sorrow, pain, and loss she'd held back since the explosion at the mine.

She was tired. Tired of being strong. Tired of going on as if nothing had happened. Tired of everything.

Sucking in the last of the sobs, Elizabeth drew herself upright, smoothed back her hair, and straightened her back. One slow step at a time, she walked through her home. Everywhere she looked, reminders of Steven and their life together brought more tears.

"Steven, what am I to do?" she asked, picking up the framed wedding picture. "The money from the mining company has only gone so far. What is left may not be enough to sustain our home for long."

Tracing the face of her husband's image with a trembling fingertip, Elizabeth swallowed a trembling sigh. There was only one thing she could do to keep their home—her home.

Surely someone in Blessings Valley would have clothing in need of mending. She'd go back to being a seamstress and do what she must to survive.

"Yes, that's what I shall do. It may not be much, but if I'm frugal, I may not have to give up our home." Elizabeth set the picture back on the mantel, a small smile on her face that didn't reach her heart.

Gathering a black shawl around her shoulders, Elizabeth stepped out of her home and onto the road leading to the heart of Blessings Valley. This was the first day in weeks since they'd put Steven in the ground that she'd left the sanctuary of her home. She'd only gone to get supplies, avoiding as many people as possible.

The warmth of the day did little to her warm her cold and broken soul. The late morning was as quiet as new fallen snow, much like her spirit.

Placing one foot in front of the other, Elizabeth strolled slowly along the path. She paused for a moment in front of the small church she and Steven attended often. Her gaze travelled up to the cross hanging above the door, and she closed her eyes.

How could a God she worshipped take her husband and those of her friends? One day she may find enough forgiveness to walk through those doors again, but she'd never forget. She'd never forget the pain the loss of her precious love caused.

Turning her back on the church door, Elizabeth continued on her way to Smith's Dry Goods. She would need to purchase thread in several colors and needles of different sizes if she was to return to work as a seamstress. She'd once been very handy with a needle and thread—before Steven had swept her off her feet, married her, and brought her to Blessings Valley where they started to build their life together. That was five years ago when the mine first opened.

Those days were long gone, and that life a ghost of her past. The reality of being alone was a bitterness she now was learning to live with, like it or not.

"Elizabeth!" Willa Alexander called from her

front porch, a broom in her hand.

Why can't I just go to town without seeing anyone? Elizabeth put on her well-practiced brave smile and waved. "Willa, how are you?"

"I am fine." Willa leaned the broom against the railing then took one step down the planked stairs. "Please, do come in for some coffee. I could use the company today. The last of the boarders is gone, and the house is overwhelmingly quiet."

"I am on my way to Smith's," Elizabeth answered, then saw the crestfallen look sweep into her friend's eyes. "But it can wait until after a cup of coffee."

"Please, do come in!" Willa chanted, opening the door to her boardinghouse. "I think I may even have a muffin or two left from breakfast."

Elizabeth lifted the front of her skirt, slowly walked up the several wooden steps onto the porch, then followed Willa into the boardinghouse's front parlor.

"I'll be back in a moment. Please do sit and make yourself comfortable," Willa said, sweeping her hand toward the seating arrangement in the parlor then scurrying to the kitchen.

The room was simple and rich with dark red wood. Books overflowed the shelves of three bookcases. A large grandfather clock ticked away the minutes of the hour in a corner.

The parlor, while masculine, held the touch of a woman in its fine yet simple cream French shawl drapes and lace doilies on each table. The wallpaper was a French gray, giving the room a welcoming warmth.

The ornate fireplace was void of a fire, its hearth free of soot. Perched on the mantel along with other knick-knacks was a picture of Willa on her wedding day.

Elizabeth's heart stuttered with the new knowledge that she too would survive Steven's death, just as Willa had survived her husband's passing years ago.

For a brief moment, hope warred with despair. Part of her wanted to go on as she knew Steven would want her to. Yet, how could she when the love of her heart was no longer with her to share life with?

How was she to live a fulfilling life without her husband to share it with her? She didn't even have a child, their child, to love that would have been a part of Steven.

She was virtually all alone. That's what her heart had been saying for near a month now.

"Well, we are in luck!" Willa chirped, carrying a tray of two cups, a steaming pot, and a plate of muffins into the parlor. "There was even some honey left for the muffins."

Elizabeth smiled then took a seat next to Willa on the settee. "This is very generous of you, Willa."

"I wasn't sure when you'd last eaten," Willa said, pouring coffee for the two of them. "I wanted to visit you, but you have saved me the walk."

"I was going to Smith's to replenish my sewing box." Elizabeth took a sip of her coffee when all she wanted to do was tell her friend not to worry about her. That she'd be fine and didn't need her well-intended sympathies.

"I thought maybe I could earn some extra money doing mending for people." Elizabeth put her cup down and stared at the muffins, wondering why she'd just revealed her situation to Willa. Oh well, the entire town would find out soon enough anyway.

"Do you mind if I come with you? I noticed that I am in need of a bag of cornmeal," Willa asked, her eyes full of a hope Elizabeth didn't have the heart to squash, no matter how sad she herself was.

"Of course! I am grateful for the company." Elizabeth lied cheerfully, wanting nothing more than to be left to herself.

WILLA DRAPED HER shawl over her shoulders as she walked through the doorway with Elizabeth. She'd made a promise months ago to seven souls, and Willa was going to keep that promise one way or another. It was time she kept that vow, and she was going to start with Elizabeth Hamilton.

Although the widows needed a bit of time to themselves, she knew what these poor young women had been going through. She also knew it wasn't preventable; they'd have to go through it all in order to come out the other side of grief a different person.

When Charlie died, Willa wouldn't accept help from her friends or her family. She only wanted to hide away from the outside, believing her world had come to an end. And in many ways, it had, only to open a new one. In time, Elizabeth would accept help and find her way to a new world. Until then,

Willa would give a gentle push to that path.

Willa and Elizabeth walked into Smith's side by side. The cowbell loudly clanked their arrival, and Mr. Smith popped up from behind the counter.

"Good morning, Mrs. Alexander, Mrs. Hamilton." Mr. Smith nodded, dusting his hands off. "I trust you ladies are doing well."

"Good morning, Mr. Smith," Willa answered, going straight to the back where the bags of cornmeal were shelved. "It is a beautiful morning! Don't you agree, Elizabeth?"

"Oh, yes. Yes, it is," Elizabeth mumbled, her hands already buried among the spools of thread.

Willa smiled at Mr. Smith, placing a five-pound bag of meal on the counter. "Please charge this to my account, Mr. Smith. Thank you."

"Of course," Mr. Smith said in a hushed voice, watching Elizabeth as she rummaged through the once neat rows of thread. "Is she—"

"Yes, and thank you, Mr. Smith," Willa answered in a low, discreet voice, then strolled over to Elizabeth.

"I think your idea is a splendid one," Willa said in a quiet voice.

Elizabeth looked at Willa through squinted eyes then returned to the task her fingers were performing. "You do? I thought you'd be the first one to try and discourage me."

"No need to look at me like I'm a bug you need to squash!" Willa laughed as Elizabeth continued to shuffle spools of thread from the table to her basket and back to the table again. "I'm sure there must be lots of mending needed at Nana's Laundry. That would be a good place to offer your services."

"I would think they have someone to do the mending; it is a laundry after all," Elizabeth commented, placing another spool and package of needles into the basket.

"Maybe, but I cannot imagine they would have anyone as skilled as you are," Willa said, taking Elizabeth by the elbow. "Let me help you, Elizabeth, please. You can post something at the boardinghouse if you'd like."

"Thank you, Willa." Elizabeth blinked back the tears Willa saw surface. "I am grateful for your offer, but—"

"I am happy to give it, Elizabeth." Willa patted Elizabeth's arm, saying, "We girls have to stick together."

"Yes, I suppose we do." Elizabeth sighed, then methodically placed her purchases on the counter.

"That'll be –" Mr. Smith began.

"Let me get this," Willa began then, seeing her mistake by the look on Elizabeth's face, pulled back her offer of monetary help. "No, of course not."

"Thank you, Willa, but I have to learn to stand on my own two feet sometime. I still have some money to live on. I'm not totally destitute. Besides, I have many items that need mending that I've been putting aside," Elizabeth said, handing the money for her notions to Mr. Smith. "Thank you, Mr. Smith. You always have such a variety of threads, I'm sure I'll be back for more."

"You ladies have a nice day!" Mr. Smith called out as they walked out the door.

Willa looped her arm through Elizabeth's,

halting her in the street. "You can call on me for help anytime, Elizabeth. For now, I'll put a notice up for boarders who need some mending."

"No, Willa," Elizabeth stated. "I won't start taking charity from people. Especially not my friends. And since my family is far away, there is no one except myself to depend on. I will find my own customers, Willa. Please, I know that it is something only I can do—for now anyway."

"Yes, Elizabeth," Willa stated firmly. "However, I insist that you allow me to help you. You know I'll do it anyway, so why not just accept my help?"

"Goodness Willa. I can see there is no convincing you otherwise," Elizabeth stammered, giving in to her. "I shall accept your offer, but only if I can pay you for the advertisement."

"Agreed!" Willa smiled as they walked the short distance back to her boardinghouse.

ELIZABETH KNEW WILLA only wanted to help her. But she didn't want her, or anyone's, help or sympathy or pity. She only wanted her Steven back; while her heart protested he was forever gone and not coming back, her head kept telling her this was her new reality—life as a widow. Eventually, her heart might believe her head, but not today, or tomorrow, or ever, as far as she was concerned.

"Willa, I'm sorry if I have offended you in any way." Elizabeth took her friend's hand in hers, giving it a light squeeze before letting go. "It's just that—well, I don't—why is it so hard for me to express myself? I can't seem to find the right words anymore, not since…"

"Let's sit on the porch a while before you go home," Willa suggested, guiding her up the steps and over to the end of the porch where a swing and small round table sat.

Elizabeth settled down on the porch swing, fighting the tears threatening to overtake her once again. They seemed to come at the most unexpected times, especially when she felt she was at her strongest. Like a summer thunderstorm, there they would be—unexpected and furious. As long as she was alone, she'd let them fall, but she would not allow herself to give in to them in front of anyone. Nor would she give in to the pity in the eyes of people who watched her struggle not to let them fall. She wouldn't allow it! She had to be strong for both herself and Steven.

Willa sat down beside her, and Elizabeth fought the urge to put her head on Willa's shoulder and let the tears come. What good would it do anyone? Not one bit, that's what! She'd keep telling herself that until it was true.

"When my Charlie died, I locked myself in our room for days," Willa began, covering Elizabeth's hand with her own, as if she were looking for her own strength. "I'd go through his things over and over again, hoping to find something that would make him walk through the door and take me in his arms like he used to do."

"Willa, you don't have to—"

"Yes, Elizabeth, I do," Willa said, turning to face Elizabeth. "If I must tell my story over and over again, I will.

"Charlie Alexander was one of the richest young men in Marion County. And he wasn't the boy I first fell in love with, but that is another story altogether." Willa sighed, her gaze off somewhere Elizabeth felt she was intruding on.

"But Charlie was charming, and before long, he won me over. We had a happy life together, and I was very blessed to be his wife. His loss almost undid me, and if not for a very persistent family, I might not be in Blessings Valley. I might be out in the cemetery next to Charlie.

"So, you see, Elizabeth, no matter what you say or how much you try to push me aside, I will always be here." Willa squeezed her hand, and Elizabeth felt a tear slip from her eye.

"I know I'm not alone. That I'm not the only, nor the first, woman to lose her husband." Elizabeth swiped at the tear, picked up her basket of notions, and stood. "You then can understand, above all others, that this is something I must do on my own. In my own way, and in my own time."

"Yes, I do." Willa stood, taking her into her arms. "I am here for you and the others. All you have to do is call on me. Promise you'll do that."

The basket suddenly feeling like a bunch of bricks, Elizabeth gazed into Willa's pleading eyes. Her heart exploding from the love—and sorrow— she saw laying in their depths. How could she not make a promise to someone so generous? So caring? Elizabeth could not.

"I promise to call if I need you." Elizabeth hugged Willa then headed for home and to an empty house.

CHAPTER 2

"Blast!" Augustine Raines grunted, wiggling his fingers through the bottom of the pocket in his suitcoat. "Nothing lasts forever, not even a hundred-dollar suit made by the best tailor money can buy."

Disgusted, Auggie shrugged off the coat, tossing it on his neatly made bed. Opening the wardrobe, he yanked another dark-colored coat off a hanger.

"If this keeps up, I'll need an entire new set of suits." Auggie slipped the garment on then looked in the mirror, making sure he was presentable. Satisfied all his flaws were hidden, he left his apartment for his office two floors down in the Grand Hotel.

The mining accident had brought in welcome business. The hotel had been full for several days with the arrival of families, government inspectors, and newspaper people. It also brought back a memory that always lay just below the surface of his mind.

His own disfiguring accident. A silly bet on a horse race between himself and an old friend. Auggie's horse had stumbled, and he landed unconscious against a tree. Not only had he lost a rather large bet that day, but his face had been torn wide open along the jawline from his chin to his ear. The doctor had done the best he could to minimize the scarring, but Auggie felt he looked like a scarecrow. His once clean-shaven face now sported a neatly trimmed beard hiding the ugly scar behind it.

The incident had done more than disfigure his face; it had also made him leery of any woman who gave him any kind of attention since. In his mind, he was positive it was his money they were after, because, after all, why would a woman want a damaged man? One that would be hard to look at, even with the light low. For that reason, he'd decided to leave high society and set out for Oklahoma Territory when the opportunity to open the hotel came his way.

No one here knew of him. They only knew he was having a hotel built. They didn't know he was a rich man. Here, in Blessings Valley, he could escape the debutantes trying to latch onto his bank account.

And he had accomplished his goal. It was lonely, but that was the price he was willing to pay to not have to worry whether or not he was loved for the man he was.

So, he lived the life of a confirmed bachelor.

"Good morning, Mr. Raines," Stewart, the desk

clerk, called out as Auggie reached the bottom of the stairs. "We are a little less than half capacity this morning. Several of our guests have gone to the bakery to wait for the stagecoach."

"Thank you," Auggie said, acknowledging his employee. "Please have breakfast brought into my office. I have an appointment with Mrs. Alexander this morning."

"Yes sir. Your usual, Mr. Raines?"

Auggie nodded. "Yes, and please show Mrs. Alexander in the moment she arrives."

Auggie went into his office where he already had the hotel files on his desk. He couldn't imagine what it was Willa wanted to see him about. Her boardinghouse was doing well, taking clientele that couldn't afford the Grand.

Even though she was his competition, Auggie liked the widow. She was the type of woman who didn't mince words, she just came right out and said what she thought.

Auggie knew Willa wasn't the least bit interested in more than a friendly business relationship, and that suited him just fine. He wasn't in the market for romance of any kind.

"Mr. Raines, Mrs. Alexander has arrived," Stewart announced, pushing open the partially opened door.

Auggie dismissed his thoughts, then stood. "Mrs. Alexander, please do come in."

"Thank you." Willa smiled, strolled into his office, then sat in the chair opposite him.

"Please have Cook hold breakfast until after Mrs. Alexander and I have concluded our business."

Auggie nodded to Stewart then took his seat again as the door softly closed. "What can I help you with today, Willa? You aren't here to discuss our agreement, are you?"

"No, far from it," Willa said, her gaze taking stock of him.

He felt like that little boy in the boarding school being inspected by the schoolmaster when Willa's gaze traveled over him. His hand sought out the spot on his breast pocket where her assessing eyes lingered.

Blast! How did I miss another tear?

"Looks to me like your suit is in need of some repair, Auggie," Willa commented, continuing to assess him with a small grin on her face.

Was she really passing judgment on him? What gave the boardinghouse owner the right to have any opinion on his appearance? Even if they did have a business agreement of sorts.

"So, it seems to be my lucky day. I've already changed suitcoats once this morning before coming down for the day." Auggie shrugged, doing his best to hide the embarrassment creeping through him. "I'll have to go up to my apartment as soon as our meeting is over and change again. I'm starting to run out of suits that don't need mending of some sort or another." He laughed.

"Yes, you may. But I do have an eye for such things. Maybe no one else will notice," Willa suggested.

"The point is that I'll know," Auggie retorted, feeling the need to rush upstairs that very minute and discard yet another damaged suitcoat. "Shall we get down to the business that has brought you in this morning?"

"I know it is rather sudden, and there's a good reason that has nothing to do with the boardinghouse or our arrangement." Willa smiled. "It has to do with helping out one of the widows."

Auggie sat back in his chair, rolling a pencil between his fingers. "I must warn you against loaning money to anyone who may have a difficult time repaying it. I do sympathize with their losses, but I'm not sure what can be done for them."

"I wouldn't dream of insulting them by offering a loan, and none of them has asked for one," Willa answered.

"That's good, so what is it then?"

"Imagine that you have a hotel guest who discovers she needs a seamstress as one of her dresses has been damaged during her trip. Where would she find one?" Willa leaned in toward him, her eyes back on the rip. "Would she have to resort to making the repair herself? Call on Nana's where she'd have to take the garment there herself? Or could she just call on the Grand Hotel seamstress to mend the dress?"

"If the hotel had such a seamstress, I'd direct said guest to her. As it is, that service isn't offered here at the Grand." Auggie tossed the pencil on his desk, wondering what sort of scheme Willa was cooking up this time.

"But it could be." Willa smiled, obviously holding her secret scheme on the tip of her tongue.

It's just like a woman—keep secrets to use later. Willa has never wanted anything from me before, so why now? Might as well hear her out or she'll not leave me to get on with today's business.

Intrigued, Auggie looked down at the rip in his jacket than back over to Willa. "Please do go on, Willa."

"I BELIEVE YOU are in need of a seamstress for yourself, if not the hotel guests." Willa smiled. At least she'd gotten his attention, and he seemed to be interested in what she had up her sleeve. She was sure of it.

"Yes, we've already established that unfortunate need." Auggie chuckled, shrugging his shoulders.

"Did you know there is a fine and very capable seamstress right here in Blessings Valley who could take care of that mending for you?" Willa asked, knowing full well that he didn't. It wasn't something Elizabeth would have shared with the hotel owner. She wouldn't have had any reason to. As far as Willa knew, she was the only one who knew and that was by pure accident.

"No, I didn't. And please don't stretch this out. Willa, just spit it out," Auggie strongly suggested.

She had a mind to keep him on the hook, but knew he might spit out the bait she was offering and break the line.

"Typical man, always in too much of a hurry to listen to what a woman has to say," Willa snorted, shaking her head. "You already know Elizabeth Hamilton is one of the widows. But what you may not know is that Mrs. Hamilton was a seamstress before she married Steven Hamilton."

"Yes, I do know of Mrs. Hamilton, and no, I don't know anything about her past. Why would I?" Auggie said, crossing a leg nonchalantly over a knee. "I don't make it my business to know the past lives of the women of Blessings Valley. And most certainly, not married ones!"

"She's a widow," Willa reminded him. "So technically, she's not married in the eyes of the law nor God."

"Nor widows either, as they were once married," Auggie declared. "What have you got up your sleeve, Willa?"

"Mrs. Hamilton is a strong-willed woman. The type of person who won't take any handouts, not even from me." Willa hoped she wasn't pouring it on too thick. She didn't want to scare the catch away. "To put it bluntly, she needs employment before her money runs out, Auggie."

"Why not hire her at the boardinghouse?" Auggie asked. "I'm sure some of your boarders would have more than enough to keep her busy. After all—"

"She refused to accept my help," Willa interrupted, pursing her lips. "She wouldn't even let me hang a flyer up without taking payment first." Even though she admired Elizabeth for her refusal, Willa was still miffed she hadn't accepted her help. Yes, she certainly did admire Elizabeth Hamilton's desire to find her own way. Just not her reasoning for denying any.

She only needs a small push in the right direction, Willa thought. *And Auggie has been alone far too long, for whatever reason.*

"I was thinking that the Grand may be in need a seamstress, and by the look of things, there is a need for her services." Willa nodded at Auggie's tear in his suitcoat.

"I'll have to think about it," Auggie said, tenting his fingers against his chin.

"Don't think too long. After I leave here, I'm going straight over to the Gold Star. I'm sure the girls there could use Mrs. Hamilton's skills." Willa sat for a moment longer watching the expression on Auggie's face change as he soaked in her false declaration. Sighing in exaggeration, she stood, smoothing down her skirts.

"While you continue to take it under consideration, Auggie, I'll be determined to find that widow some honest work. I only hope it'll be with a reputable business so her reputation isn't tarnished." Willa turned and strolled toward the office door.

Come on, Auggie, do the right thing. She put her hand on the doorknob and turned it slowly. Pulling the door open, she took a step out of the office and away from the hope she'd had in Augustine Raines.

"Willa, wait!" Auggie called.

Willa let go of the breath she'd been holding, turned off the instant smile on her face, then turned back around. "Yes, what is it?"

"Since Mrs. Hamilton won't take charity, how do you propose getting her to work here? I can't very well walk up to her and say that I am in need of her services; I might get slapped," Auggie said, pacing behind the desk, stroking his beard.

"I have a plan. Are you willing to hear it?" Willa stood in front of Auggie, her heart rejoicing that she'd chosen correctly.

"Yes, yes, of course, I am. Please sit down and tell me how I'm going to get a seamstress for my hotel." Auggie finally stopped pacing and sat back down.

"It's quite simple, actually," Willa stated, pulling out the folded piece of paper that she'd tucked into her small bag before leaving the boardinghouse. "I took the liberty of writing an advertisement. All you have to do is walk over to *The Chronicle* and place it."

Willa handed the paper across the desk to Auggie. "I hope you approve. As you will see, I also took the liberty of quoting a proposed salary."

Auggie read the advertisement, raising his eyebrows. "This is quite generous. There isn't any proof of Mrs. Hamilton's skills, except for her word."

"Regardless, she's worth every penny, Auggie." Willa said, turning to leave. "I guarantee it."

"WHAT HAVE I gotten myself into?" He shook his head, pushing the paper aside, as Willa Alexander walk out of his office with a spring in her step.

Shaking his head, he picked up the paper written in Willa's hand and re-read the simple advertisement for a seamstress. It was straightforward. The Grand Hotel was in need of a seamstress. The position would be as needed and offered a generous hourly wage.

He'd acted out of character when he'd responded rather quickly and without weighing the costs. Something he hadn't done since his accident. At least this time around, the possibility of landing unconscious against the trunk of a tree with his face ripped open was slim. He may have the reputation of being cold-hearted, which he didn't think he was. He just wasn't looking for a wife.

No matter. He wouldn't have been able to look at himself in the mirror, knowing he'd allowed Willa to find that poor widow work at the saloon. He could only imagine the pain these women were going through, coping with their heartbreaking losses.

So why not hire Mrs. Elizabeth Hamilton? At least until she got on her feet, however long that might take. As long as it wasn't more than six months.

Until then, the hotel could benefit from having a seamstress available for the guests. Some of what Willa said did ring true. And judging from the condition of his suits lately, he was in need of those services as well. Being the loner that he was, approaching a woman in town to do the repairs wasn't within his scope of reaching out. Having a seamstress here at the hotel would save him from either doing the mending himself or sending it back East for repairs to the only tailor he trusted with his custom-made suits.

Auggie stood, folded the piece of paper, grabbed his derby, then headed out of his office and to the lobby.

"Are you ready for your breakfast now, Mr.

Raines?" Stewart asked, looking up from his work.

"No, I'm afraid not. Please tell Mrs. Hall I'm sorry." Auggie paused at the desk, fingering the brim of his hat. "Stewart, might I ask you a question?"

"Yes, of course. What can I help you with, Mr. Raines?" Stewart replied, surprise written in his eyes. It wasn't often—if ever—Auggie asked the opinion of his employees.

"Since you are the person most of our guests have contact with during their stay with us, have any of them ever inquired as to whether or not the Grand has a seamstress on staff?" Auggie wanted to know how much of his money he would be throwing away by hiring Mrs. Hamilton. If he was right, it would be more than he'd want to waste his money on.

"As a matter of fact, yes," Stewart answered.

"Honestly? How often?" Auggie asked, taken aback that it was a service requested. How had he not thought of it before Willa's suggestion of hiring Mrs. Hamilton? He'd never thought that people staying over for a day or two would need such a service.

"May I be blunt then, Mr. Raines?" Stewart placed the pencil precisely in the middle of the ledger in front of him.

"By all means. It seems the word of the day is blunt, so speak your mind." Auggie snorted, placing his hat on the desk. He had a feeling this wasn't going to be quick.

"If you are considering hiring someone," Stewart began, "I would recommend it. Over the past week alone, there were several requests for repairs. I had to send them down to Nana's, only to have them return with their garments not mended. Seems the laundry doesn't take in any clothing for repairs only. So, they returned disappointed and the damaged garment in hand."

"And if there had been a seamstress here, those situations could have been avoided." Auggie unfolded his hands from behind his back.

"Yes, sir." Stewart nodded.

Auggie knocked his knuckles on the top of the desk. "I'll be out for a time. Thank you, Stewart, for being candid."

Settling his hat on his head, Auggie set out for *The Chronicle* to place his ad. Seems the Grand was going to have its very own seamstress.

CHAPTER 3

Elizabeth pulled several folded bills out from the can she kept hidden under a floorboard in the pantry. She'd had several days to consider Willa's offer and decided she wasn't going to accept it. Not willingly anyway. She didn't want people to think she couldn't do for herself. That all she was looking for was someone to hold her hand. She'd never been that kind of person before and she wasn't going to start now.

She'd spent the last few days going over an advertisement to place in *The Chronicle*. With so many people coming through town, as well as the town's residents, someone had to be in need of some mending.

As much as she respected Willa, valued her friendship, and was grateful for her wanting to help—well, Elizabeth knew she needed to stand on her own two feet. At least, that was what she kept telling herself over and over and over again.

And after much discussion with her Steven, that was what she was doing, starting today.

Elizabeth paused at the fireplace on her way out of her house and, as she so often did, gazed at their wedding picture.

"Steven, I'm going to place the advertisement. It's the only thing I can do." Her eyes misted over. She sucked in a shaky breath. "I will not let them see me cry. I will be strong for both of us."

Shawl wrapped snuggly around her shoulders, Elizabeth began on a journey she thought she'd never have to take.

"You can do this, Elizabeth. You have to." She muttered softly, putting one foot in front of the other along the path she knew all too well.

"Hi, Elizabeth!"

Looking up, Elizabeth's gaze settled on the open church door, and a warm shiver slipped down her spine. Fannie Rochester, who'd lost her husband the same day Elizabeth had lost her Steven, stepped out into the morning sun.

"Hello, Fannie," Elizabeth called back, biting her tongue when all she wanted to do was lash out at Fannie. How could she find solace in church when God had taken their husbands from them?

"Won't you come in and sit with me?" Fannie offered, stepping closer.

"Not today, Fannie, thank you." Elizabeth waved as she continued on her way. She would never forget the pain of losing Steven. Not now. Not ever.

"Maybe I should move into Willa's boardinghouse, so I don't have to pass the church ever again," Elizabeth mumbled. Feeling her heart race, stealing her breath, she paused for a moment. "Go ahead, take me to join Steven, and I will go willingly." She took deep breaths until her heart returned to its normal cadence then continued on her way.

Elizabeth rounded the corner leading into the heart of Blessings Valley. She loved this little mining community that had become home. The thought of having to leave it broke what was left of her already shattered heart. If she didn't find work soon, she'd be on the first stage at the end of the month.

"Good morning, Elizabeth." Willa's voice sounded like the chorus of a song. "Care to join me?"

"Hello, Willa. Not right now, thank you for your kind offer. I have an errand to do, and I mustn't be late." Elizabeth smiled, waving. "Have a good day, Willa."

"You also, Elizabeth." Willa sounded overly gay for so early in the day with a quiet boardinghouse at the moment.

She's up to something, I can feel it, Elizabeth thought, passing the rest of the businesses unscathed on her way down to *The Chronicle*.

Elizabeth's steps slowed when she reached Smith's Dry Goods. She'd gone too far to turn back now, *The Chronicle* office was next.

You can do this. You know you can.

The words floating through her mind sounded like Steven's voice. A reminder of who she was. She was Steven Hamilton's widow, and she was strong. She would carry on as Steven would want her to. Elizabeth knew that for a fact. She wasn't about to let Steven, or herself, down.

Drawing in a breath of courage, Elizabeth stepped through the doors of the newspaper office.

"Mrs. Hamilton." Clint Wagner looked up from his printing press, his hands smudged with black ink. "What brings you in this morning?"

"Mr. Wagner, I'd like to place an advertisement." Elizabeth laid the paper she'd been clutching on the counter. "In your next edition, please."

"It won't be until the end of the week, Mrs. Hamilton. Tomorrow's issue is almost ready," Clint informed, wiping his hands down the stained apron around his waist.

"It will have to do." Elizabeth's words rang with the disappointment she felt inside. She shouldn't have weighed her words so heavily before acting on what she knew she had to do.

"What are you selling, Mrs. Hamilton?" Clint took only a few steps before reaching the counter and glancing down at her neat handwriting.

"Looking for work, not selling anything," Elizabeth said, watching for disapproval while Clint read her notice.

"You're a seamstress?" Clint asked, raising an eyebrow.

"I used to be, before Steven and I were married," Elizabeth said softly then gathered herself together to continue. "Now I need to go back to it, or I'll be forced to leave Blessings Valley for good."

"I think I might have something for you." Clint wiped his fingers with a somewhat clean cloth, a grin on his face.

"You have some mending that needs to be done?" Elizabeth asked, a small hope rising in her.

"No, Mrs. Wagner would not be too happy if I hired someone to do what she's been doing all these years," Clint chuckled.

"Oh, yes, of course." Elizabeth's rising hopes dashed, and she felt her soul sinking toward the floor to be stomped on.

"But the Grand Hotel is looking for a seamstress." Clint looked up.

"It is?" Elizabeth asked, surprised by her luck.

"Mr. Raines was here a few days ago and placed the ad. It will be in this edition I'm printing." Clint put the rag down, returning to his printing press.

"The Grand Hotel," Elizabeth pondered, feeling her spirit lifting. "Thank you, Mr. Wagner. I think I'll go see Mr. Raines right away. And please, hold my advertisement for now."

AUGGIE SAT BEHIND his desk, going over the books for the month with little success. His mind kept wandering back to the advertisement due to be in tomorrow's *Chronicle.*

What if Elizabeth Hamilton didn't see the advertisement in the paper? What if every other woman in town did and they showed up at the hotel? Then what was he to do? Tell them all they weren't what the hotel was looking for? That their qualifications weren't enough? Turn them away?

He'd be shooting himself in the foot if he did that. He had a reputation to maintain with his employees.

He probably should have just gone to see the woman and offered her the position instead of listening to Willa. From what she'd said about Mrs. Hamilton, the widow probably wouldn't have taken his offer, thinking it a handout.

Well, the ink was dry, and he'd see it through, no matter who contacted him for the position. At least for a month or two. If business was slow and not profitable, maybe shorter.

But if it turned out profitable, he might have to invest more into it. The hotel could sustain the extra cost if business continued to flourish.

"Mr. Raines?" Stewart inquired, standing just inside the door.

"Yes, Stewart, what is it?" Auggie looked up from the financial ledgers he'd been reviewing.

"There's a woman here, regarding a seamstress position." Stewart's brow furrowed in question. "Is there such a position?"

"The notice doesn't appear in *The Chronicle* until tomorrow," Auggie said, more to himself then to his desk clerk. Sitting back, he pondered the situation for a moment. Had Willa informed Mrs. Hamilton that he was looking for a seamstress? Had she also told the widow that it was at her insistence that he do so? Only one way to find out—have the woman come in. But what if it wasn't Mrs. Hamilton, then what was he to do?

"Did she give her name by chance?" Auggie asked sitting forward over his desk.

"I believe it's one of the widows; Mrs. Hamilton, if I am right."

"But you aren't sure?" Auggie tapped the pencil lightly on the ledger.

"No, Mr. Raines. I didn't ask her name." Stewart cast his gaze downward, shaking his head. "She only asked to see the person in charge of hiring for the seamstress position. I didn't think to ask her name. I was certain that she was mistaken."

"It's all right, please send her in," Auggie instructed, closing the financial ledger.

Stewart nodded then left to go into the lobby, where Auggie presumed the woman waited for him. When he returned, it was with a pretty woman in her late twenties, dressed in a dark plain dress, long auburn hair pulled back, and the saddest blue eyes Auggie had ever seen.

"Mrs. Hamilton is here to see you, Mr. Raines," Stewart announced escorting Elizabeth Hamilton to one of the wingback chairs.

Auggie stood, blood rushing through him. "Mrs. Hamilton, please do sit down." He noted the way his heart raced the moment his gaze met hers. "What is it I can help you with?"

"If I may be straightforward, Mr. Raines. I need a job, and I understand you have a position for a seamstress available." Elizabeth spoke in a brave, matter-of-fact tone. Her gaze never wavering from his, he couldn't help but feel drawn to her.

"Yes, that is true. May I ask how you found out?" Auggie asked seeing past the false façade. He admired her bravery for trying to move forward with her life.

Willa said Elizabeth Hamilton was a strong woman, and now Auggie believed her. Under that bravery she showed everyone was a woman who loved deeply. Not sure why, but he knew it in his heart.

"Purely by accident, I can assure you, Mr. Raines." Elizabeth smiled, nervously fingering the clasp of her handbag. "I happened to be at the newspaper office to place a notice for my services as a seamstress. Clint Wagner told me that the Grand Hotel had placed an advertisement for one in tomorrow's edition. So, I came over right away."

Auggie watched her for a moment. He saw the sorrow she was trying to conceal. He thought it bordered on the desperation of a woman struggling to survive on her own.

"Clint is correct, of course. I am considering taking on a seamstress as a service to the hotel guests." Auggie studied her face carefully. Something about her continued to draw him in with each passing moment, and he wanted to help her as much as he could. "Are you qualified?"

"It has been several years, but yes, I believe so," Elizabeth said, a small glimmer of hope in her eyes. "I was a dressmaker at a small dress shop back in Virginia. When Steven and I married, I continued my skills from home until we came here to Blessings Valley."

The sadness in her voice reminded Auggie of the days after his father had passed. His mother, trying to get through that first year. She had made it through the grief with the love of family.

It sounded like her family was back East.

Blessings Valley was all she had to guide her through the pain and grief of losing her husband. The people of Blessings Valley were her family now. And that included himself.

"Mr. Raines, I need this position. Not only financially, but for my own sanity. I need to feel useful." She nearly begged, tears in her eyes.

"Your sanity?" Auggie thought it was an odd phrase to use for a grieving widow. Did she think she was losing her mind?

"Maybe it was too strong of a word to use. I want to stay in Blessings Valley. I can't if I don't have a way to support myself." She glanced down then looked him in the eye. "I believe you hold the only hope I have, Mr. Raines. I am very capable of doing an honest days' work, for an honest wage."

Relief swept through Auggie. He didn't need, or want, a hysterical woman on his hands, no matter how much Willa Alexander tried to convince him otherwise. He believed Elizabeth Hamilton was indeed desperate but not hysterical. The woman's honesty pulled at him. Clearly, she was in need of financial assistance, yet instead of conniving or asking for a handout, she would only accept help if it came in the form of a job.

"Mrs. Hamilton, if you are willing to start tomorrow, then I am offering you the position on a trial period. Are you agreeable to that?"

"MR. RAINES, AS you know, I am in a position that enables me to start tomorrow. I'm sure you also know that my late husband was one of the men who died in the mine explosion months ago." Elizabeth clutched her bag to keep from shaking.

"Yes, Mrs. Hamilton, I am truly sorry for the loss of your husband. And I am aware of your situation. Or I imagine you wouldn't be looking for work," Auggie said. "But that doesn't change the fact that your employment is on a trial basis. And for the books, I will not make any exception because of your situation."

Sitting back in his chair with a smug look on his face that Elizabeth found both annoying and adorable, which also annoyed her. She blinked back the tears in her eyes caused by his bluntness. He may appear a hard man, but there was a softness in his eyes that told her otherwise.

When she came to see about the position, she hadn't expected a trial period. She'd expected to be permanently hired. She'd been bold enough to think that her word regarding her experience would be enough.

Now, she'd have more to worry about. What if she didn't work out? What if one day he decided he didn't like her work? Or worse yet, her?

"I'll prove myself and my skills to you. I promise you won't be disappointed, Mr. Raines." Elizabeth drew in a breath to steady her nerves. She needed this job. She needed the money in order to stay. Not only in Blessings Valley, but also in her home. "How long is the trial period?"

"Thirty days, and I'm sure you will work out, Mrs. Hamilton." He stood, looming over his desk. "Now, go home for the day and try not to worry about your future for now. I ask that you be here by eight in the morning."

"Thank you, Mr. Raines. I am truly grateful that you agreed to see me before your advertisement came out." Elizabeth extended her hand to her new employer. As soon as their hands touched, something sizzled though her so quickly, she wasn't sure if she'd felt what she thought she'd felt. "I'll see you in the morning then. Good day, Mr. Raines."

Elizabeth quickly smiled then turned and took a few steps before she heard the chair scrape on the floor.

"Oh, one more thing, Mrs. Hamilton," he said.

"Yes?" Elizabeth turned to see Mr. Raines coming around his desk, brows furrowed. *Has he changed his mind?*

"Would you mind bringing your sewing box with you? I'm afraid I haven't had time to get all the supplies you may need. This is somewhat embarrassing since I've now hired you. Truth be told, I'm not exactly sure what is needed by a seamstress, other than needles and thread that is. And I'm sure there's more to just patching up a seam than those two items. I've always sent my suits out in the past for any repairs." His face turned a deep red. "I'm sorry, I know how that must sound. However, I promise to replace your private notions if there is a need to use them. Tomorrow, we will go to Smith's and get as much as you need."

"I'd be happy to, Mr. Raines. I'll fix that tear in your suitcoat first thing in the morning, as well." Elizabeth eyed the frayed edge on the lapel of his suit. "Thank you for having faith in me, Mr. Raines." Elizabeth smiled, walking out of the office door.

Once she reached the street, she took a deep breath and restrained herself from doing a jig. She had a position! Now, she'd be able to support herself, at least for the next month. For that, she was grateful. Spending the money to buy needles and thread the other day was a wise decision, even if she thought it unwise when she'd gotten home.

The first step was to cancel her notice for Friday's newspaper on her way home. Then maybe she'd stop for a few minutes and tell Willa there was no need to put up notices in the boardinghouse as per their agreement.

To think she might have missed this opportunity if she had waited until tomorrow to come into town. Through all her doubt about placing the advertisement and the days perfecting it had led Elizabeth to becoming the first seamstress at the Grand Hotel.

Was this the opportunity she really wanted? Judging by his "sent his suits out" comment, was he the type of man who looked down on his employees? Or was he a rich man who happened to own the Grand Hotel? He had those kind eyes; how could she think he'd be a tyrant?

She would definitely stop at Willa's on the way home after all. She'd know if she was making a mistake or not. Not that it mattered because Elizabeth had made the commitment for at least the next month. Enough time for her reputation as a seamstress to get around town, and then she could start her own business in her home.

"Yes, that's it. A chat with Willa will ease my

nerves," Elizabeth said, stepping back into *The Chronicle*.

CHAPTER 4

Auggie stood in his office doorway watching Elizabeth Hamilton walk back out into the street. This woman was different from the debutantes he'd known. She wanted no one but herself. She wanted to do things on her own. And by God, Auggie knew that Elizabeth would eventually be a force to be reckoned with.

And for some reason Auggie couldn't fathom, he found that aspect of her quite appealing.

"Stewart?" Auggie stepped out into the lobby and over to the door, his gaze on Elizabeth as she strolled toward the newspaper office.

"Yes, Mr. Raines?" Stewart called out, coming down the hall from the kitchen with a tray of breakfast food.

"Let it be known that the Grand Hotel now has a resident seamstress." Auggie smiled, turning toward his desk clerk.

"We do?" Stewart said, surprise radiating in his

eyes, the plates rattling on the tray.

"Yes, we do." Auggie chuckled, taking the tray from Stewart's hands before the young man dropped it. "I'm afraid I've made more work for you and the staff. I will need to have one of the storage closets emptied and fixed up for Mrs. Hamilton. Put any nonperishable items stored there up into the attic until they are needed."

"Yes, sir," Stewart said, his mouth all but gaping open.

"And make sure there is a comfortable chair, as well as a worktable or small desk. Also, the lighting must be bright enough for her to see while she is mending," Auggie instructed, grinning as he walked back toward his office. If he wasn't careful, he'd be having pretty wallpaper hung in the closet to brighten the small area up.

"How soon do you need this done, Mr. Raines?" Stewart asked, following Auggie into the hotel office.

"By eight in the morning." Auggie placed the tray on his desk, savoring the smell of bacon and eggs. His stomach rumbled in response to the thought of what lay on the plate under the still-warm dome. "I'm sorry for the short notice. But I am confident you will have the task completed by then."

"Yes, sir." Stewart nodded, his gaze on Auggie. "Where shall I get the furniture from for this room? There may be some things in the attic."

"Good question." Auggie mulled it over for a moment. "Not the attic. I don't want to take the chance that anything up there might be in need of repair. I should think one chair and a small table would not be missed from the dining hall. As well as a good lamp to see by."

"I believe that is possible. I do have an idea that may work," Stewart offered, his brows raised in question. "Would the storage room off the dining room be sufficient? It does have two windows that would provide daylight. I could set up the table and chair near the west window."

"Yes, I think that will do quite well." Auggie sat in the chair behind the mahogany desk, hands folded in his lap. "Thank you again, Stewart. I knew I could depend on you."

Auggie smiled, slid forward in the chair, and poured cream into his coffee. He heard his door click softly as Stewart left him to mull things over.

Despite himself, Auggie found Elizabeth Hamilton comely and very pleasant. Mostly, he thought there was a woman hiding inside her that was stronger than she seemed. The kind of woman he would have swept off her feet at one time.

Those times were long past. He wasn't open to a relationship, possibly love, only to be turned away once his disfigurement was revealed.

The Grand Hotel's seamstress would be nothing more than an employee. Plain and simple.

ELIZABETH LIFTED HER skirt and jogged up the steps of the boardinghouse. Knocking on the door, she paused a moment before walking into the parlor.

"Willa!" she called out, her heart pounding against her ribcage. She hoped her actions wouldn't give away her excitement. She wanted to hold on to the moment of joy for herself a bit longer.

"In the kitchen," Willa answered, the sounds of pots clanging in the background.

Elizabeth walked through the dining room to the back where the smell of freshly baked bread grew stronger with each step. The kitchen was small but functional, and Willa appeared to be at home there.

"Oh my! That is the best smell in the world," Elizabeth exclaimed inhaling deeply then setting her chatelaine bag on the small table for two.

"I was about to have a late breakfast. Would you like some?" Willa asked, wiping her hands down the front of her apron. "I've got honey and sweet butter, as well as preserves. And a fresh pot of coffee to wash it all down with."

Elizabeth nodded in agreement as she took a seat at the corner table. Willa cut a few slices of bread and poured them each a cup of coffee. Elizabeth watched, remembering the joy such a simple act gave her on the mornings her Steven was home. For once, a memory that didn't cause sadness in her heart.

"Did you get your errands taken care of?" Willa asked, smearing honey on her buttered bread. "You were certainly in a hurry earlier this morning."

Elizabeth took a slice of bread for herself, trying her best to maintain her composure. It was more difficult than she thought it would be, keeping a happy secret. Every fiber in her was jumping with joy. She hadn't felt joy in so long.

"I did, in a way." Elizabeth poured a spot of

cream then dropped one cube of sugar into her cup, stirring the contents until the coffee turned a light caramel color.

"Did something happen?" Willa asked, slowly placing her bread on the plate. "Are you all right? You seem to be, but if something has happened, you can tell me. Maybe I can help; listen, if nothing else."

"I'm fine, Willa. I couldn't be any better right now." Elizabeth took a bite, then placed her slice of bread onto her plate, dusting off her fingers. "I was in a rush this morning, and I apologize if I was rude to you; it was unintentional. I went to place an advertisement in the paper this morning. That's where I was going when you stopped me. When I got there, Mr. Wagner was already printing tomorrow's edition."

"Oh, I'm so sorry, Elizabeth. I know you must have taken your time in perfecting that notice." Willa reached across the table, patting her on the hand. "You can put it up here, you know that."

"Yes, I know. There's more to tell. I did miss that edition. It could go into the next one, but that won't be until Friday." Elizabeth took a sip of her coffee, watching Willa over the rim of her cup.

"Clint read over my advertisement," Elizabeth continued, setting down the cup. "He told me two very interesting pieces of news."

"What were they?" Willa had a worried look on her face. "Were they good or bad?"

"A bit of both." Elizabeth feigned a scowl, sighing loudly. "The first was that my notice wouldn't appear until Friday. The second was that the Grand is hiring a seamstress and their notice is going to appear in tomorrow's paper."

"Elizabeth! How splendid and lucky for you. It's a wonderful coincidence," Willa exclaimed, a twinkle in her eye. "Did you go down to the Grand and inquire? I had been watching for you, wondering if I'd missed you returning home or not."

"Yes, I did." Elizabeth smiled, feeling quite proud of herself. A month, even a week ago, she wouldn't have done such a bold thing. "And Mr. Raines hired me for a thirty-day trial. If he likes my work, then I can only presume he'll offer me the position permanently."

Willa shot out of her chair and around the table before Elizabeth could blink an eye.

"This is wonderful, Elizabeth!" Willa pulled Elizabeth into a hug, squeezing her gently. "This calls for a celebration. I'm positive he'll hire you on permanently. He'd be a fool not to."

"Wait, Willa." Elizabeth laughed, all the worry of how she was going to survive faded away. "I have a number of things to do in preparation. I need to go through my sewing box and discard any weak thread. And I also need to mend a couple of my own dresses if I am going to look presentable to customers—and to Mr. Raines."

"I will bring you down something later then," Willa offered, a tear slipping down a cheek.

"Willa, are you all right?" Alarm crept through Elizabeth. She'd never seen Willa shed a tear—not even at the funeral for the miners. "What has happened? I was so enthralled with my own joy that

I didn't notice something was wrong."

"Oh, Elizabeth!" Willa laughed, swiping at the tear. "I am so happy you are on this path, that is all."

"So am I, Willa." Elizabeth picked up her bag and strolled through the dining room. "Now you won't have to put up that notice for me after all. I owe you so much," she said, squeezing Willa's hand. "You are a good friend, Willa. Blessings Valley needs you. I need you."

Elizabeth hugged her friend, then bounded down the porch steps, and headed for home.

"STEWART, PLEASE GATHER the staff and have them come here to the lobby. We are having a quick meeting," Auggie instructed, pacing the floor in front of the hotel doors.

"Yes, Mr. Raines." Stewart walked away with an urgency in his step.

Auggie had made it a practice to keep the hotel staff aware of any changes. And the addition of a seamstress was big enough that he wanted to squash any gossip that may follow when the news broke that he'd hired one of the widows before the newspaper came out.

Mary Hall was the first to arrive, her hands folded in front of the apron hanging from her shoulders. She was his longest and most faithful staff member, having arrived days before he'd opened the doors. Auggie's mother was none too happy that Mary had followed him from her kitchen to his.

"Augustine, is everything all right?" Mary

asked, stepping into his path. "You seem a bit tense."

"Do I?" Auggie stared at her, then blinked. "Everything is fine, Mrs. Hall; you'll see."

Mary smiled then walked over to the lobby desk as James Butler and Lee Johnson, the hotel bellboys, and Stewart joined them. They all stood quietly watching him, waiting with controlled anticipation.

"I can fetch Sally, Mr. Raines. It won't take but five minutes," Stewart offered, a crooked grin on his face.

Sally Jenkins, the hotel maid, had gone home earlier after her duties were completed. Auggie had a suspicion that Stewart had more than a passing interest in her, judging by his eagerness to get her.

"No need, Stewart. You can take a note to her later this afternoon." Auggie smiled, rocking back on his heels.

"Now, I'm sure you are all wondering why I called you together." Auggie clasped his hands behind his back to keep from sticking them in his front pockets. A social mistake his father drilled into his head at a young age every time he was caught with his hands in his pant pockets.

"There is going to be an advertisement in tomorrow's paper. It will indicate that the Grand Hotel will be conducting interviews for a seamstress." Auggie continued pacing and looking down at the carpet to hide the uncustomary smile on his face. "While this is true, the position has been filled this morning, quite unexpectedly."

"Was it the young woman I noticed this

morning?" Mary asked, a twinkle in her eye.

"As a matter of fact, yes, it is." Auggie smiled, meeting Mary's amused gaze. "It's one of the recent widows. Mrs. Hamilton comes well qualified, and I expect great things from her.

"Stewart will need help moving items from the storage closet adjacent the dining room to the attic. James and Lee, I trust you'll assist him with whatever he needs.

"Once the room is emptied and looking presentable, Stewart will move one of the armchairs, a small sawbuck table, and a lamp from the dining room into the former closet. Stewart and I have briefly discussed how to set up the room to fit Mrs. Hamilton's needs. Once that is done, I'll make any adjustments, then approve the arrangement.

"Now to ease your minds, the hotel can manage an extra employee on payroll. Mrs. Hamilton will be working a thirty-day trial period, for now. I know you will all make her feel welcome at the Grand."

"When will Mrs. Hamilton begin her duties?" Mary queried, that twinkle back in her eye.

Evidently, something was pleasing her. Did she have some dresses that were in need of repair? Doubtful. Mary would make the repairs herself, not pay someone to do it.

"At eight o'clock tomorrow morning," Auggie answered, looking at each of the staff. "Now, if that is all, there is work to be done."

Stewart gathered James and Lee, and the trio left the lobby in a flurry through the dining room.

Mary hung back until they were out of hearing range.

"I'll have breakfast ready for her. No reason for her to start on an empty stomach." She turned to go back into the kitchen. Pausing for a moment, she looked back at Auggie, a big smile on her face and a tear in her eye. "You've done a good thing here, Augustine. You're a good man, don't you ever forget that." And with that, she left him alone in the lobby.

Auggie smiled, shaking his head. Mary had always seen the best in him since he was a little boy. But she was right. Somewhere between two damaged suitcoats and hiring Elizabeth Hamilton, his world seemed a little brighter.

CHAPTER 5

Elizabeth pulled her hair up, twisting it into a bun. She was excited and a bit nervous. Starting her position at the Grand Hotel today had led to a restless night. This was the first major step she'd taken in getting on with her life and her new social status.

Widow.

She hated the word and all that it implied. What a lonely sounding label and frame of mind. It conjured up the image of an angry, lonely woman who may never love again. Who may have lost her way on the dark path of grief. And while Elizabeth may never love another man again, she would live her life to its fullest and try to be kind and caring to everyone she met.

After returning home from Willa's yesterday, Elizabeth had immediately set about inspecting the condition of her various threads. She'd just replenished her supply of needles, so there was no need to purchase more. At least not until one broke.

For the next thirty days, she'd show Mr. Raines how frugal she could be by saving the hotel some money—no matter how small the amount. She didn't want to give him any reason for not taking her on permanently.

Standing over the table, Elizabeth made herself a sandwich of butter and preserves for lunch, then grabbed an apple, dropping both into a sack. They were things she could eat quickly without spending much time away from her work. And she wouldn't have to spend any of the money she'd put away on lunch. Until she had a steady income, she wasn't about to spend what little she had for eating at work when she had the makings of a sack meal in her kitchen.

Rechecking her sewing box for the tenth time, Elizabeth glanced at the mantel clock. Seven o'clock. One more hour before she had to report in at the hotel. What would she do with herself over the next thirty minutes?

Elizabeth paced the floor, feeling like she should be doing something. She was too worked up to sit and wait. She'd been up since dawn getting ready. Making sure that she was presentable. She wanted so badly to make a good impression on Mr. Raines. Her life in Blessings Valley depended on it.

"I can't wait any longer. I'm going to leave now, Steven, but I'll be back later today." Elizabeth spoke to the wedding picture as she did every day. Talking to it was her way of feeling connected with her beloved in her mind, as well as in her heart.

Shawl around her shoulders, sewing box in her

hand, Elizabeth walked out her door and down the steps. The sack lunch she'd prepared sat on the table where she'd left it, but it was far from her mind as she passed the church.

The door remained closed this early. The rising morning sun shone brightly on the stained-glass windows, the panes colorful and mesmerizing.

Her heart and soul might be slowly mending but not enough to walk through those doors again. Ignoring the invitation the message in the windows offered, she continued on her way to the hotel, a slight heaviness claiming a spot in her heart.

Elizabeth strolled into town, the promise of a new day wrapping around her. It was still a bit too early for most of the businesses to be open. She saw Vera Baldwin duck into the door at Nana's Laundry. Poor Vera was another of the widows who'd lost her beloved in the same accident that had claimed Steven.

The Baldwins had been in town for less than six months when the explosion happened. Elizabeth realized she was luckier than Vera. Yet like Vera, Elizabeth also found herself employed and alone, fighting for her place in Blessings Valley.

"Stop with these sad thoughts. They won't do you a bit of good!" she scolded herself, shaking her head. "You are so much braver than you believe, Elizabeth Hamilton."

"Elizabeth!" Willa waved from her front porch, broom in hand. "Good luck today."

"Thank you," Elizabeth called back, waving. *Doesn't she ever sleep?*

By the time Elizabeth reached the front steps of

the Grand, Blessings Valley was waking up. Shades were being drawn up in the windows. Closed signs flipped to open. Front porches and steps swept off.

It was going to be a glorious day!

AUGGIE TUGGED ON his vest, nervously gazing at his image in the mirror. He'd meticulously trimmed his beard and mustache earlier this morning. Inspected the rest of his suitcoats until he found one free of damage. Satisfied with his appearance, he went down to his office, arriving well before seven o'clock.

He'd gone to look over the seamstress room one last time. A small table sat under the window where it would give the best light during the day. A lamp on a corner would provide adequate light on cloudy days. And the chair would provide comfort for those long hours Mrs. Hamilton sat while making repairs for guests.

Yes, this room was perfect.

Unsure as to whether or not she would have eaten, his next stop was the kitchen. Mary was already preparing breakfast for the few guests sitting in the dining room.

"Good morning, Mrs. Hall," Auggie greeted, pouring himself a cup of coffee.

"Augustine," she said, stirring pancake batter.

"Would you be able to fit in a breakfast tray for Mrs. Hamilton this morning?" he asked, snatching a warm biscuit from the breadbasket. "Maybe some of your delicious pancakes, eggs, and biscuits. A pot of coffee would probably be nice as well."

"Of course, I can," she answered, pouring

batter onto a sizzling griddle. "In case you hadn't notice, she needs to put on a bit of weight, too skinny for my liking."

Auggie coughed, nearly choking on a piece of biscuit. "Um, no, I hadn't noticed."

And he hadn't. Looking at Elizabeth Hamilton in any other way than as an employee would be inappropriate.

"You need to pay attention, Augustine." Mary turned to him, pointing a spatula at him. "The poor widow has probably been scrimping and not eating properly. You don't want anyone walking into her room to find her slumped over that table now, do you?"

"No, ma'am." Auggie smiled, brushing his hands off on a towel. "Can you bring in some breakfast about 8:15 then, please?"

"Yes, now get out of here before those guests waiting to eat go to the café," Mary scolded, turning back to flipping the pancakes.

Walking down the hall, Auggie glanced at his pocket watch, and his heart thumped in his chest. Seven-thirty. Elizabeth Hamilton would be here in precisely thirty minutes.

"Good morning, Stewart." Auggie glanced at the desk clerk, walking over to the front doors. "Please show Mrs. Hamilton to my office when she arrives."

"Ah, Mr. Raines?" His head down, Stewart flipped open the guest register.

"Yes, what is it?" Auggie stepped around the desk and headed into his office.

"Mrs. Hamilton arrived a few minutes ago."

Stewart looked up, trying to suppress a grin. "I showed her to the sewing room."

"What? She's here already?" Auggie's step slowed, and he turned around. "I wasn't expecting her for another thirty minutes."

"Would you like me to bring her to your office now, Mr. Raines?" Stewart asked, hiding the grin Auggie saw creep on his face.

"No, I'll go see her myself." Auggie turned toward the dining room which lead to the sewing room. "Thank you, Stewart."

Walking through the dining room, Auggie nodded at the few guests waiting for their breakfast. Reaching the back of the room, he stood inside the open doorway where a very light scent of lavender lingered.

Elizabeth stood looking out the window. A sewing box sat open on the table. Her shawl was draped across the back of the chair.

Auggie hesitated for a moment, admiring the silhouette. Back straight, hair pulled back in a bun, she appeared to be deep in thought, as if she were somewhere else.

Taking a step back out of the room, he drew in a breath, tapped on the door, then entered.

"Good morning, Mrs. Hamilton." He greeted her cheerfully.

She turned, a small smile on her face. "Good morning, Mr. Raines. I came in early. I hope it isn't an inconvenience to you."

Inconvenience? Why on Earth would she feel coming in early would be an inconvenience?

"Not at all, Mrs. Hamilton." Auggie stepped

into the room. "Are the accommodations suitable for you to work?"

"Oh yes, they will do nicely." When she turned fully to face him, he glimpsed the dried trail a tear had left. "I am very grateful, Mr. Raines. You have no idea what it means to me to have this chance to—" she turned her attention to the sewing box, fiddling with the contents "—make a living and to be able to stay in Blessings Valley."

"I think I do, Mrs. Hamilton." Auggie stepped closer to her, wanting to put an arm around her. To tell her that she was an important part of the hotel now. That if she needed anything, he'd do his best to help her.

What the heck was he thinking? It was too soon to tell her anything remotely like that, let alone think it. And he had no business thinking about holding her close. None whatsoever!

"Mr. Raines, where would you like the tray?" Mary asked as the wondrous smell of breakfast filled the room.

Auggie jumped out of his skin. Turning to Mary, he half expected her to see the thoughts in his head. If anyone could see through him, it was Mary. Sometimes he thought she knew him better than he knew himself. She certainly knew him better than his own parents had.

"In here, if Mrs. Hamilton has no objection," Auggie said, feeling lighthearted when Elizabeth nodded her approval. "Wonderful, I will get myself a chair. I think this room could use two after all."

Auggie relieved Mary of her tray then went into the dining room to retrieve another chair.

ELIZABETH POURED COFFEE into each of the cups as Mr. Raines left for a chair. She stood looking out the window, catching glimpses of Blessings Valley and its people.

Her people.

Her family.

She belonged here, and thanks to Mr. Raines, she'd be staying.

"You haven't had your breakfast yet, have you, Mrs. Hamilton?" Mr. Raines asked as a matching chair was brought in.

"I had some bread and preserves. Unfortunately, I accidently left my sack lunch on the table." Elizabeth felt the heat warming her cheeks and turned away. "I was in such a hurry this morning that I walked out the door without it. With your permission, I'll go home at lunch then immediately return."

"Mrs. Hamilton, may we get a few things out in the open?" Mr. Raines asked, pulling one of the chairs closer to the table and tray of food.

"Yes, of course. I believe in honesty, Mr. Raines." She sat in the chair as Mr. Raines held it for her. It had been a while since a man held her chair. The last time was when—well, it had been Steven who'd done so the night before the explosion. Her heart slammed against her breast at the memory of their last meal together.

"Good, that pleases me." Mr. Raines replied sitting in his chair. "Let me make it clear that as long as you are employed at the Grand, you will never have to be concerned with bringing a lunch or eating breakfast during a workday. Mrs. Hall would have my hide if I didn't offer to feed the employees."

"Mrs. Hall?" Elizabeth asked, raising her eyebrows. Who was this woman who had so much influence on Mr. Raines? "Is she the lady who brought the tray in?"

"Yes, she's been with me for as long as I can remember." Mr. Raines smiled, and it somehow softened his features. "Mrs. Hall is the hotel cook, and while she runs a tight ship, she is the kindest woman I know."

"I see," she said, watching him closely as the emotion he had for Mrs. Hall came and went quickly. She noted that his trimmed beard of yesterday looked to be trimmed even more. She had a feeling that the round wire-rimmed glasses she hadn't noticed yesterday were a hiding place for him. She was sure of it, judging the reservation that lurked behind them. "What else do you wish to be honest about, Mr. Raines?"

He scooped some egg onto his fork then slid it into his mouth. "If you don't mind, I suggest we eat while talking. Is that acceptable to you, Mrs. Hamilton?"

As if he needed her permission to eat. He was her employer—he could eat anytime and anywhere he wished.

"It is, Mr. Raines." Elizabeth picked up a warm biscuit, spreading preserves on it.

"I would like to be your first customer." Mr. Raines looked at her over his cup, his gaze expecting nothing more than acceptance.

"Of course. Might I start with the unfortunate

rip in the suitcoat you wore yesterday? I believe I have thread that would match the material perfectly." Elizabeth pulled a dark blue spool from her sewing box, holding up the spool for him to inspect.

He chuckled. "I was thinking of that one as well. I also have a lighter brown one that has a pocket in need of repair. I brought them both down with me this morning to my office."

"If there is nothing else, I am ready to get to work on them then." Elizabeth placed her fork and knife on her empty plate. If she didn't start doing something, she was afraid her full stomach would lull her to sleep.

"I shall retrieve them and bring them into you after I return the tray to the kitchen." Auggie stood and began gathering the dirty dishes onto the tray.

"Mr. Raines, if you would allow it, I would very much like to return the tray to Mrs. Hall." Elizabeth was surprised at how much she'd eaten. Mrs. Hall's breakfast had been a feast she hadn't had after several months of pinching pennies. She wanted to convey her appreciation of a wonderful start to a new day. "I will pick up your suitcoats on my way back."

"As you wish, Mrs. Hamilton. I shall see you in my office shortly." Mr. Raines nodded, then left the room as quietly as he'd entered thirty minutes ago.

Elizabeth finished placing the dishes on the tray then followed in Auggie's footsteps, satisfied that the Grand Hotel would be a fine place to work.

And Mr. Raines a wonderful and kind employer.

CHAPTER 6

Elizabeth carried the breakfast tray into the kitchen where the woman she presumed to be Mrs. Hall stood over the stove. She was humming catchy a tune Elizabeth hadn't heard before.

"Mrs. Hall?" Elizabeth asked, stepping over to the small table for two in the corner. "Where would you like me to put these?"

"Yes?" Mary turned with an instant smile that turned to confusion in a flash. "Goodness, right there on the table is fine. Why didn't Auggie bring those back? I'm going to have to speak to that boy."

"I told Mr. Raines I would bring them back. It gave me something to do before the two repairs I have to work on." Elizabeth set the tray onto the table then picked up the soiled dishes and carried them over to the large sink. There was no reason she couldn't take care of her own breakfast dishes, especially since she hadn't paid for the meal. She would pull her own weight, refusing to take advantage of Mr. Raines's generosity. "Mrs. Hall, who is Auggie?"

"I'm sorry, I was too familiar. Auggie is Mr. Raines's first name." Mrs. Hall dropped several cut-up chicken parts into the steaming pot, followed by an array of herbs and spices. "Chicken stew for lunch today with buttermilk biscuits. I'll bring you some around noon, if the dining room isn't too busy."

"That isn't necessary. I can come get my own lunch. I don't want any special treatment, Mrs. Hall. I'm not used to being waited on. It doesn't feel appropriate here somehow." Elizabeth wondered about Mrs. Hall.

When had she come to Blessings Valley, and how did she know Mr. Raines? What was their relationship? Was Mrs. Hall a widow as well? Or did she have an absent husband who traveled on business? Or did she only pretend to be married as so many unmarried women of her age did to keep unwanted suitors away?

"Mrs. Hamilton, I have wanted to tell you how terribly sorry I am about your husband," Mary said softly with a deep kindness that took Elizabeth by surprise. There wasn't any pity in her words. They were edged with genuine sorrow. And her eyes held a knowledge most wouldn't understand. What it was like to be alone. "You girls are far too young to be widows."

"Thank you, Mrs. Hall." Tears sprang to Elizabeth's eyes. She swallowed away the rock of grief threatening to choke the life out of her. "Is there a Mr. Hall?"

"Oh, not for many years. I am thankful we had a full life together. I have so many happy and loving memories that carry me through any dark moments." Mary smiled, her eyes bright with those memories she eluded to. "And of course, I had the Raines family to help me through the grief."

"The Raines family?" Elizabeth asked, surprised by this small piece of information. Was Mrs. Hall somehow related to Mr. Raines? No, she wouldn't be working as a cook in his hotel if she was. What was her connection then? "You know Mr. Raines's family?"

Mary laughed, adding flour and stirring the now simmering pot. "Yes, for a long time. I've known Auggie, Mr. Raines that is, since he was a young man. By his silly youthful actions, I'd say a boy, really. He has done some rather questionable things through the years that he has had to pay for."

"He seems to be pleasant." Elizabeth meant it, but what in his past had he done to make him feel responsible for? "He is kind in taking me in as the hotel seamstress before today's papers were delivered. Of course, I have Mr. Wagner to thank as well; he told me about the position."

"Auggie is a kindhearted and compassionate man, if a bit guarded." Mary turned around, a bit of sparkle in her eye. "But I sense that is all going to change. Now, run along, dear, so I can finish my work here. I don't want what guests we have heading down to the café."

Elizabeth smiled then wandered slowly down the hall toward the lobby where Mr. Raines's office was nestled behind the registration desk. She'd promised to pick up his suitcoats on the way back from the kitchen to repair them. Hopefully, she'd have more than just those two pieces to work on today. If not, it would be a long day of sitting around sorting thread. Or a very short one, and she'd be home earlier than she'd anticipated.

AUGGIE LOOKED OVER the notice announcing the hotel's need for the services of a seamstress. Stewart had tactfully sent away the few interested applicants who had arrived then promptly put a sign in the window announcing the position was filled.

Maybe Auggie should have put up the notice yesterday after he'd hired Mrs. Hamilton. He certainly hadn't expected to see her in his office before the paper was published.

What was done was done. Truth be told, Auggie was pleased with having hired her. True enough, it had all happened quickly. He hadn't had time to digest it all with transforming the storage room into a sewing room. It was small for now; if business mandated it, then he'd find a larger room.

Then, when he saw her this morning standing in the light of the window, something moved inside him. He couldn't identify it or put a name to it. He felt it through his soul. As if she was there waiting just for him, Auggie. Not Mr. Raines.

But it wasn't so. Mrs. Hamilton had been waiting for Mr. Raines.

"Excuse me."

As if she knew his thoughts, Elizabeth stood in the doorway of his office.

"Mr. Raines, I've come to get your suitcoats

now," she said waiting patiently while he foolishly stared at her.

"My suitcoats. Ah yes. I have them right here," Auggie stuttered, pushing out of his chair. Walking to the door, he reached behind it, pulling down the garments in need of repair, then handed them to her.

"I believe I have a matching thread for this one," Elizabeth commented, inspecting the dark jacket, then turning to look over the light caramel one." I don't think I have anything that would blend well with this one. So that may be a problem."

Auggie took the lighter jacket from her, looking it over. Smiling, he placed the open jacket on his desk. With scissors, he snipped a piece of fabric from inside.

"Mrs. Hamilton, I believe it is time to make a few purchases over at Smith's." Auggie chuckled. "Please get your shawl and meet me at the front door."

Nodding, she left the office. Auggie stuffed the piece of material into his pants pocket, put his bowler hat on his head, and walked into the lobby just as Mary appeared.

"Going somewhere, Auggie?" she asked, a mischievous twinkle in her eye. "You never leave the hotel this time of day. Must be important to have you rushing off."

"Yes. Mrs. Hamilton and I are going for a few things she needs." Auggie kissed her lightly on the cheek. "And don't get any romantic notions, Mary."

"Remember, you're a gentleman, Auggie." Mrs. Hall smiled then turned back to the hall as Elizabeth strolled gracefully into the lobby.

"Let's go then." Auggie offered Elizabeth his elbow. She hesitated for a moment then took it as they walked out the door and down the steps into the street.

They walked the short distance over to Smith's in silence. Once inside the dry goods store, Auggie handed her the swatch of material. As she looked through the spools, he retrieved a few personal items.

After only a matter of minutes, she joined him at the counter with several thread options in her hand.

"One of these will work fine. I'll know for sure which one once I start the repairs." Elizabeth placed the spools next to his other items.

Auggie looked up at Mr. Smith, amused by the look on the man's face. *The rumor mill will be grinding away by the time it's dinner if I don't clarify why Elizabeth and I are together. I hate having to explain myself or my actions. But I have her reputation to think of, not mine.*

"Mrs. Hamilton is employed at the Grand as its new seamstress. Please add her name to the hotel account so that she may acquire what she needs in the future," Auggie said, signing the credit slip.

"Yes, sir, Mr. Raines." Mr. Smith nodded, making a note on the hotel's account book.

"Thank you." Auggie offered Elizabeth his elbow again as they left the dry goods store with the purchases.

"You do realize this is going to get all over Blessings Valley before the end of the day." Auggie patted her hand, just before it slipped away.

"I hadn't thought of that. In the future, we must not step out together like this again. You are my employer, Mr. Raines." Elizabeth spoke so low, he had to tip his head toward her in order to hear. "It isn't proper for you to appear too friendly with your employees. Especially if they are female—and widowed."

"Yes, you are right, of course. I was raised that a gentleman should always escort a lady, you see, and that's only what I am doing. Even if said lady is my employee," Auggie explained as they neared the hotel. "However, there is one thing I must insist on, Mrs. Hamilton. With your blessing, of course."

"What is that, Mr. Raines?" She gazed up, her eyes sparkling with wonderment.

"Please call me Auggie. It would be easier than Mrs. This and Mr. That. With your permission, may I call you Elizabeth?" Auggie held his breath for a moment, waiting for her to say yes, hoping that she'd agree.

"The way I see it, I'm your employee." Elizabeth gazed at him, then lowered her lashes. "Since you asked, you may, but only when no one else is present."

"Of course, Elizabeth." Auggie agreed happily as they entered the hotel and parted ways in the lobby. He was surprised how her name rolled off his tongue with natural ease.

A few hours later, Auggie smiled all the way back to his office from the seamstress's room with his suits draped over an arm. He liked Elizabeth. She was a determined and self-sufficient woman. There were no society airs about her one bit.

Willa Alexander had given him a gift when she suggested taking on Elizabeth as a seamstress for the hotel. Her personality was gentle, and her skill in repairing garments was amazing.

He could barely see the stitches she'd made. No one would notice unless they were close enough to actually inspect the stitches. And there'd never be anyone that close to him, so there was no need to worry about out it. He doubted even Willa would be able to tell the difference.

His repaired coats in hand, Auggie strolled into his office, whistling. The tune was as cheery as his mood.

"Mr. Raines, are you all right?" Stewart asked, concern on his face. "Should I get the doctor? Or Mrs. Hall and her tonic?"

"I couldn't be better, Stewart!" Auggie smiled, closing the door to his office.

ELIZABETH SAT ACROSS the table from a patiently waiting Willa. Waiting for Elizabeth to report on how her first day at the Grand had been.

Elizabeth sipped her tea and then smiled, placing the glass in front of her.

"Well?" Willa sat back, her hands gripping a sweating glass. The cool morning had turned sweltering as the clouds gave way to the sun and clear, blue skies.

"It went well." Elizabeth began feeling her heart warm as she pondered what to say next. "Mr. Raines is a soft-hearted, kind man. His staff seem eager to please him and are equally as nice. Mrs. Hall, the cook, knows quite a bit about Mr. Raines."

"And the work? Was there any for you today?" Willa poured more tea into their glasses then offered Elizabeth one of her famous coconut cream cookies.

"No, thank you. I am full after eating Mrs. Hall's cooking. She made a hearty chicken soup with biscuits for lunch." After months of scrimping, Elizabeth had not felt this full after eating only two meals in a day.

"Yes, she likes to make sure no one leaves the table hungry." Willa chuckled. "Was there any work for you today? Or did you only eat all day?"

"I'm sure you've heard the gossip by now, Willa." Elizabeth felt warmth seep into her cheeks. Why should she be embarrassed for having taken Auggie's elbow when he'd offered it? He was only being a gentleman, nothing more.

"You mean the one of you hanging onto Mr. Raines's arm? Yes, I have. I know there is a logical explanation for it even though the busybodies in town may think otherwise since you are recently widowed." Willa huffed. She never did have much use for gossips, and Elizabeth was right there with her on that feeling. Which was why she wanted to explain the situation to someone who would listen and know it was the truth.

"There is. Mr. Raines brought me two of his suitcoats in need of repair." Elizabeth concentrated on the amber liquid in her glass, afraid her friend may see more than what was there.

"I bet I know which ones." Willa laughed, nodding her head. "Go on, Elizabeth."

"Anyway, I needed a matching thread for one

of them." Elizabeth took a sip of tea, smiling to herself. The new memory of being on his arm brought comfort to her soul somehow.

"That doesn't explain how you ended up on his arm, Elizabeth. If I'm to stop the tongues from wagging, I need the facts." Willa waved her finger in the air at her.

"Oh Willa, it was very innocent. He offered me his arm as we left the hotel and walked over to Smith's. Mr. Smith had been giving both of us that look. You know the one that makes you feel like you're doing something wrong. On the way back, I refused his arm, but Mr. Raines took my hand, placing it at his elbow. He told me that he was raised to be a gentleman, and he would remain so, regardless of what anyone thought." Elizabeth sipped more of the cool tea to hide the grin threatening the corners of her mouth.

"Very noble of him, Elizabeth. He decided that it was more important to be respectful than to give in to idle gossip," Willa observed, grabbing a cookie off the plate. "And did you repair his coats?"

"Of course, I did!" Elizabeth gushed, aghast that Willa would even have to ask such a question. What did she think? That once they returned to the hotel, that she'd get her things and run home like a little girl? She was far from a little girl. She was a grieving widow who had known love and kindness at one time in her life. "When we got back, I took the jackets to the sewing room and set out repairing them. I doubt even you would be able to tell the difference."

Both laughed aloud as Willa gathered up their

empty glasses and crumb-filled plates.

"I guess that says it all then, Elizabeth. Unless there is more."

"More? No, there isn't more," Elizabeth reassured, not mentioning that Auggie and she agreed to be less formal with each other whenever they were alone. It didn't seem important enough to mention.

"I must go, Willa. Thank you for the tea." Elizabeth rose then gave her friend a hug. "I have things to do at home."

"Are you returning to the sewing room at the hotel in the morning?" Willa asked.

"Yes, I made a commitment to a thirty-day trial. I'm a woman of my word." Elizabeth squeezed her friend's hand then left the boardinghouse.

She strolled peacefully along the pathway. It had been a glorious day. She found she enjoyed being out among people again. The hotel staff were both generous and friendly, making her feel she'd been a part of their lives for a long time. Even Auggie had made her feel—how did she feel?

As if out of habit, her steps paused at the church for a moment. Compelled to look up, the sun lowering in the west illuminated the cross on the roof. She shivered as a tear slipped down her cheek.

How could she ever forgive herself when she couldn't forgive God? She never should have taken Auggie's elbow this morning. People would get the wrong idea. They would think she was stepping out, looking for a man to replace Steven. And that was far from the truth. No one could ever replace her beloved husband and the love they'd shared.

Turning from the cross, she finished the short trek home. Home was an empty house filled with echoes of her life with Steven.

A house empty of the love and happiness that they'd shared for so many years.

A home where an old life was fading and a new one seemed to be taking shape.

And Elizabeth had no way to stop it from happening.

CHAPTER 7

"Has Mrs. Hamilton gone home for the day, Auggie?" Mary stood in the doorway of Auggie's private quarters, a dinner tray in her hands. He'd been so absorbed in his thoughts he hadn't heard the dumbwaiter arrive.

"Yes, she has, Mary." Auggie stood, retrieving the tray from the elderly woman. "Please come in and have dinner with me, won't you?"

Mary smiled and nodded. "You haven't asked me that in a very long time, Auggie."

"Too long, I think." Auggie placed the tray on a side table as she took a seat at the small but functional dining table. "It has been a while since you came upstairs as well. I can only think there is something on your mind."

Auggie placed a dinner plate on the table for each of them. Then he retrieved the pot of coffee and two cups, followed by the creamer and sugar bowl.

"You know those stairs have gotten to be a bit much for me the older I get." Mary smiled, pouring coffee for them both. "And since you had the dumbwaiter installed, there's been no need for me to come up to your private apartment."

"Maybe it was a mistake to have one installed," Auggie teased, taking the chair across from her. "It has made life too easy for my staff."

"If I didn't know you better, I'd give you a tongue-lashing, Augustine!" she scolded, a twinkle in her eye.

Auggie laughed, watching her slowly spoon some of the corn into her potatoes. He never could understand mixing plated food together; he preferred his food not touching and eating one item at a time. He knew it didn't make sense to others, but it did in his mind.

After several minutes of comfortable silence as they ate, Auggie put down his knife and fork, then dabbed his mouth with a napkin.

"What is on your mind, Mary? And don't tell me this is a friendly social visit. I know you all too well to believe that lie." Auggie folded his napkin back onto his lap. He took a drink of coffee, waiting for her to state why she had made the unexpected visit.

"Mrs. Hamilton seems like a very sweet woman. Wouldn't you agree?" Mary smiled, grinning at him as if she knew something he didn't. And in most cases, it was true.

Auggie sputtered on the coffee stuck in his throat. "Ah, yes, she is. And very punctual as well."

"And attractive." Mary was probably fishing,

hoping to catch him unaware of what she was up to.

"My gawd, Mary. You of all people know I have no interest in starting up with a woman. Especially a beautiful widow who is still mourning the loss of her husband," Auggie reminded her, praying she would stop this line of conversation. It was making him uncomfortable to be talking about Elizabeth in this manner with his longtime confidant.

"Beautiful, is she?" Mary smiled, sipping from her cup.

"Come on. I'm not blind, just not interested." Auggie sat back in his chair, refusing to take any more of her bait. "Elizabeth is an employee of this hotel."

"So now it's Elizabeth. How interesting," she observed, her hands folded on the table in front of her.

"Blast it, Mary!" Auggie jumped out of the chair and began pacing the floor. "Must you always look for something that isn't there?"

"When it comes to my duty and your happiness, Auggie—yes!" Mary patted her lips, a tender smile on her face. "I took an oath when you were but a young boy to protect you. To always make sure you were happy. And loved.

"What I saw today in your eyes I haven't seen since that dreaded horse race. Life has found its way back into your soul, Auggie."

"You are imagining things," Auggie protested, pointing at her from across the room.

"As you wish, but it doesn't make what I saw in you today go away." Standing, she smoothed down her apron. "I'll leave you to put the tray in the dumbwaiter. I can find my own way back downstairs."

"Mary, I didn't mean to—" Auggie was sorry for snapping at the woman who'd been his champion longer than his own parents ever were.

"I'll say goodnight, Augustine." Mary turned and left the room, but not before Auggie spotted the tears in her eyes.

He'd hurt her. Something he'd never done before in his life.

And all because Mary spoke the truth. He did find Elizabeth Hamilton a very pleasing woman.

"HELLO, ELIZABETH." VERA Baldwin called out from her front stoop, looking a bit weary.

"Vera, are you home early today? Is everything all right?" Elizabeth asked, not really knowing what time it was or what time Vera normally got home from Nana's. Elizabeth seemed to have lost track of time while at the Grand.

"No, I got done same time as usual. I had to make a stop at Smith's for a few items on the way home," Vera said, her eyes downcast. "I heard something while I was there you may want to be aware of. I know if it were me, I would want to know what people were saying about—"

"Vera, you know gossip can hurt an innocent person." Elizabeth's heart drummed quickly. Although she tried to stay clear of idle gossip, she had a feeling this piece of information needed to be heard. And most likely, had everything to do with her new position at the Grand Hotel.

"I know, which is why I feel the need to tell you what I overheard." Vera blushed slightly. "You may not like it, so I am not sure whether to tell you or not now."

"All right then, spill it, Vera," Elizabeth urged, wanting to know what it was she had to deal with in the coming days. Or weeks. Most likely months, being employed at Auggie's hotel.

"Well." Vera took the steps one at a time until she stood on the ground next to Elizabeth. "It has to do with the new seamstress at the Grand Hotel."

"Hmm, yes, well, that would be me, Vera," Elizabeth said, sucking in a breath. *So far, it's nothing but the truth. It can't be all that bad, can it? Auggie already suggested that there may be some gossip after we'd stepped out together this morning. We are employer and employee, not even friends.*

"Yes, your name was mentioned in that capacity. I am happy for you, Elizabeth. I know how good it feels to be doing something other than sitting around in a cold and lonely house." Vera looked sad and about to cry before her demeanor shifted back to being strong—on the outside.

"Go on, Vera." Elizabeth shuffled from one foot to the other. If this took much longer, she'd have to sit on Vera's stoop as the story unfolded. She didn't want to be rude, but Elizabeth just wanted to go home.

"I'll just ask you point-blank," Vera sputtered. "Did you walk over to Smith's on Mr. Augustine Raines's arm?"

So, there it was. A gentleman acting like a gentleman and the rumor mill churns.

"As a matter of fact, yes," Elizabeth answered, taking one of Vera's hands in her own. "Mr. Raines was being a gentleman. He explained to me that he was raised to escort a woman and that's all he did. Escorted me to Smith's in order to retrieve a few items needed to repair a suitcoat. He also needed to add my name onto the hotel business account. I doubt there will be any need for him to go to the dry goods, or any place for that matter, with me in the future."

"I'm sorry, Elizabeth. I should have known you weren't husband-hunting so soon, so soon after—" Tears spilled over Vera's cheeks. "I don't know why I'm so emotional."

"I miss my Steven every day, Vera." Elizabeth squeezed her friend's hand, smiling away the pain. "But that doesn't mean that life has stopped for us because we are widows."

"Do you mean that you'll marry again someday?" Vera asked, shock registering across her face. "I don't think I could ever marry anyone again. No matter the reason."

"No, Vera, I'll not marry again. Steven was my one true and only love of my heart. There isn't a man alive who could ever take his place. And I don't want one to," Elizabeth said, feeling the ache in her heart for her beloved. Where once there was fullness, now an emptiness had settled in where their love had lived.

"But you are working at the hotel as the seamstress, and Mr. Raines is a bachelor," Vera pointed out.

"I got the position totally by accident, Vera. I

had gone to the newspaper to place my own advertisement as a seamstress when Mr. Wagner mentioned the Grand was looking for one to hire. I went there straight away. Mr. Raines interviewed me, then hired me on for a thirty-day trial," Elizabeth explained, even though she felt it unnecessary to defend her actions to anyone. "As for Mr. Raines being a bachelor, I have no intention of being anything more than his employee. I'm not interested, and I'm positive he's not interested either."

"Alright, as long as you know what you are doing." Vera smiled then walked back up her stoop steps.

"Vera, thank you for caring," Elizabeth called out, a small smile on her face. It felt good to have another care about her wellbeing in their own sorrow.

Vera turned, her hand on the porch railing. "If we don't look after each other, who will?" she asked then walked back into her small but functional house.

Elizabeth stood rooted for a moment. Vera was right in many ways. They only had each other who understood the pain and sense of loss since that day. Seven women experiencing it at the same time but in different ways.

It was a bond no one else could ever understand.

AUGGIE STOOD LOOKING out the window of his hotel apartment, watching the town of Blessings Valley, except for the saloon, begin to close for the night. Had Elizabeth gotten home safely? Should he have escorted her home? Maybe he should have insisted she stay and have dinner at the hotel and then accompanied her back to her house.

"Don't be ridiculous! Elizabeth wouldn't have accepted another free meal, let alone me walking her home," Auggie murmured, shaking his head as he turned away from the window. "And I can't just walk her home without damaging her reputation."

He'd never met a woman like Elizabeth Hamilton before. She was a lot stronger than she thought by forging out a life for herself following the death of her husband. And she didn't take things for granted like some women did. She wanted to work for her place, not find someone to take care of her or give her handouts. He found that a very attractive trait in her.

Yet, if she knew the position she held had been arranged for her, he had a sinking feeling she'd leave without a thought. The last thing he wanted was an extremely angry woman on his hands.

Then her beautiful face wouldn't grace the lobby of the hotel again. Not that it mattered to him. He had the hotel's reputation to protect and hiring a widow, namely Elizabeth Hamilton, under false pretenses would give wagging tongues something to yap about.

A woman like her couldn't be interested in a man like him. A man with an ugly scar across his face. If he didn't shave, she'd never see it. He'd be able to keep his damaged face from her enchanting blue eyes. Her smile was soft and inviting, lighting up any room she was in.

"Blast it!" Auggie headed out of his apartment, slamming the door behind him. Taking the steps down two at a time, he headed straight for his office.

The lobby was quiet. Stewart stood behind the desk, going over the guest book for most likely the thousandth time of the day.

"Ah, Mr. Raines." Stewart looked up from the ledger. "I was just going over—"

"The guestbook." Auggie grinned, knowing his young desk clerk too well. He was ambitious, and he couldn't do without him.

"Actually, I was going over the tickets for Mrs. Hamilton. She has several garments to work on in the morning." Stewart's eyes gleamed with mischief. "I would think she'd prefer to do them in the order in which they arrived."

"For Mrs. Hamilton?" Auggie stammered, looking at the tickets upside down. "There are items for her to mend all ready? She's only been here for a day. This can't be, Stewart."

Stewart laughed. "Maybe you should look for yourself, Mr. Raines." He turned the tickets around for Auggie to get a better look at. "News traveled quickly after the sign was posted and applicants were turned away this morning. Some of the items aren't from the hotel guests. I didn't want to turn anyone away."

"Yes, yes, that was good thinking." Scanning them, Auggie was amazed at the number of tickets. "Fifteen? Where have you put them?"

"The only place I could think of. Mrs. Hamilton's sewing room, of course." Stewart smiled, his chest puffed out, obviously proud of taking the initiative. "I had to have James build some pegs on the wall to hang the clothing on."

"Well, please show me," Auggie instructed, his hands sweaty and blood humming.

"Yes sir." Stewart stepped from behind the lobby desk.

Auggie followed him through the lobby and into the back of the empty dining room where the sewing room was. Stewart opened the door then lit the lantern on the table, the yellow glow illuminating the room.

"Oh my!" Auggie said, hands on his hips and suitcoat tucked behind his arms. "These all came in after Mrs. Hamilton left for the day?"

"Yes, sir. Looks like hiring a seamstress was one of your more brilliant ideas, Mr. Raines. Although I must say, I did doubt the necessity for one," Stewart said sheepishly.

"Only it wasn't my idea," Auggie chuckled, turning down the lantern after taking one more look at the several items ranging from dresses to shirts to pantaloons hanging on the wall waiting for the lovely Elizabeth's magical touch.

CHAPTER 8

For the next several weeks, Elizabeth went about the business of repairing garments for not only the hotel guests, but also many of the people in Blessings Valley. Especially after Auggie had begun to take in garments in need of repair from the good people of Blessings Valley who weren't staying at the Grand. In some cases, the customer would have lunch in the hotel's dining room while she made a small repair.

She and Auggie had a friendly and amicable working relationship. Elizabeth found him to be a kind, good-natured employer. A man who was becoming a friend. Much to her surprise—and dismay.

The more time she spent with Augustine Raines, the more she found herself looking forward to each day. Those first few weeks, she'd enjoyed going to the hotel and working magic with her hands; it gave her something to focus on other than missing her beloved husband.

Then she woke one morning anxious to see not only the people she worked with, but also Auggie. Today was one of those days. And while the sensation wracked her with guilt, it also made her feel alive.

Elizabeth looked through her clothes for the perfect outfit. Slipping on the dark navy skirt and a blue-and-white patterned blouse, Elizabeth felt different. Almost joyous, if that were possible. The last time she'd put something new and colorful on was the morning of the mining accident.

A wave of betrayal swept over her. She'd vowed to love Steven till death they did part. In her mind and heart, those words of promise meant until *her* dying day—not Steven's.

Shaking the feelings away, she finished getting dressed then left for the hotel.

The sun felt warm upon her face. The air was fresh with the scent of wildflowers that grew along the path.

And the church she eagerly passed each day glowed in the morning light.

Elizabeth stood on the worn dirt path gazing up at the church. The front door stood open. She waited, expecting to see Fannie at any moment. When she didn't appear, Elizabeth took a step forward, her heart pounding in her chest.

"Fannie!" Elizabeth called out, anticipating her friend's sweet voice would answer. When none came, panic swept through her and landed like a boulder in the pit of her stomach.

"Fannie!" She cried out again, running up the

steps and into the church. Her eyes searched frantically everywhere in the sanctuary. She walked up and down the aisle, her head swiveling back and forth as she checked between each of the pews. Relief flooded her when she didn't find Fannie, or anyone else, unconscious.

Feeling the weight of fright leave her, Elizabeth looked up, surprised she stood before the altar. She gazed upon the cross. Her eyes filling with tears, she fell to her knees.

Don't be afraid, child, for I walk beside you.

A light touch upon her arm startled Elizabeth. She slowly turned her head. Fannie knelt beside her, hands folded in prayer.

"He has been waiting for you, Elizabeth," Fannie whispered, her head bowed and eyes closed.

"I thought He had forgotten me after Steven's death," Elizabeth said through the tears she hadn't realized were sliding down her cheeks. "When it was I who had forgotten Him."

"He never forgets, Elizabeth. He waits even as He is always with you. He waits for you to come to Him and pray for what you need." Fannie smiled, taking Elizabeth's hand in her own. "He always hears, even if He may not always answer."

"Thank you, Fannie, for being here," Elizabeth said, swiping away the tears and rising to feet.

The two walked out of the church together. Elizabeth walked down the steps, waved goodbye to Fannie, then continued into town.

A sense of hope enveloped her being as she strolled along the path. She hadn't felt this much peace in months. Was she beginning to forgive?

AUGGIE PACED HIS OFFICE. There was a flicker as well as a brick in the pit of his stomach. How could one be nervous and excited at the same time? Especially when that person had been raised to hide any emotion?

Since the arrival of Elizabeth Hamilton, hiding his emotion had become next to impossible. Auggie found with each passing day they spent together he wanted to know more about Elizabeth. As much as was proper for a bachelor to know about a widow grieving the loss of her husband.

Where did Elizabeth's family come from? How had she met her now-dead husband? What was her favorite color? What was her level of education? Did she have any siblings? Or was she an only child like him?

For the first time in years, he was interested in getting to know a woman on a personal level. And the realization had set him off-balance. Now that he'd decided to find out more about her, things felt to be leveling out.

"Will you take lunch in your office today?" Mary stood in the doorway, wiping her hands on a towel.

"Is it that time already?" Auggie asked, glancing at his pocket watch. Eleven o'clock, not quite lunch yet.

"No, but it has been a quiet morning in the kitchen so I thought I would check on you." Mary glanced at him, her brows furrowed.

"As you can see, I am quite well." Auggie hid his thoughts behind a smile, hoping Mary didn't see through his fences.

"Are you?" Mary asked, stepping into his office and closing the door. "Because you haven't been yourself, or at least the person I've become accustomed to seeing each day since your recovery. You've been—different. Not so aloof around the staff lately."

"Honestly, Mary." Auggie turned away, stuffing his hands into those forbidden pant pockets.

"Yes, let's be honest, Augustine," Mary snapped.

Now I'm in trouble! She never calls me by my birth name unless I've done something wrong, Auggie thought.

"Go ahead, Mary, and get it over with. What have I done now?" Auggie slid his hand from the pockets and straightened his backbone. He wanted to be ready to deflect whatever Mary was about to lash him with.

"It's not what you have done, it's what you *haven't* done." Mary stood with her arms folded in front of her, the towel dangling from a hand. "You've been walking around this hotel like a lovesick puppy."

"I beg to differ!" Auggie defended himself.,

"You can beg all you want; it won't change things. No one in Blessings Valley knows you as well as I do," she declared, her stern gaze softening a bit. "You like Elizabeth Hamilton."

"Of course, I like her. I like *all* my employees, or they wouldn't be working for me," Auggie all but huffed.

"Be that as it may, you best do something about your attraction to her, Auggie. Either keep your distance from Mrs. Hamilton or start courting her. Just make up your mind!" Mary turned and marched out of the office back to the kitchen.

"Good grief! Is it really that obvious?" Auggie mused, slamming open the ledger on his desk. Sitting with a huff, he leaned back and closed his eyes.

Would it really be so horrible if I tested the waters a little to see if Elizabeth might be interested in me? To see if there may be a chance of successfully courting her?

That would mean exposing myself to her— scarred face and all. Am I really ready for the rejection that is sure to come? Or the comments from others I have successfully been able to avoid?

Auggie scowled. A vision of Elizabeth on his arm, the two of them laughing and happy. Greeting the people of Blessings Valley openly with no harsh whispers of pity behind their backs.

Whispers of the beautiful and lonely widow and the ugly scarred hotel owner.

"MORNING, WILLA," ELIZABETH called out as she stood in front of her friend's boardinghouse. "It's a glorious day, don't you agree?"

"Why, yes, it is!" Willa answered, sweeping off the bottom porch step. "You are in a sunny mood today."

Elizabeth joined Willa on the steps of the boardinghouse. "I am, Willa. Are you free for lunch today? It has been weeks since we last really had some time to have tea."

"Of course, I'd love to," Willa replied, a big

smile on her face. "It so happens that I am free of boarders for the midday meal."

"Great. How about noon then?" Elizabeth suggested, suddenly feeling anxious to be on her way. She wanted to have plenty of time with Willa and not have to worry about the garment repairs waiting for her today.

"I'll see you then, Elizabeth," Willa agreed.

"See you then," Elizabeth said, waving as she turned and continued on her way to the Grand.

She was happy to have lunch with Willa now that something inside her had changed. Elizabeth had yet to define it and in truth, hoped Willa would be able to give her some insight on the feeling that had unexpectedly crept into her grief.

Was it peace that brightened that dark spot lodged in her heart for months? Or something else totally unexpected? Maybe she was growing accustomed to being on her own.

Whatever it was, Elizabeth wanted to confide in Willa to hear what she might think was happening. She knew she wasn't forgetting Steven or their love. How could she when theirs was a match made in Heaven? The tears and sorrow that had been present every minute of every day were subsiding. Deep down, she was afraid of losing those agonizing memories that kept her from moving forward. Because that would mean she'd moved on from losing her husband. The only forward motion she wanted was to make a place for herself in Blessings Valley. Like Willa had.

Elizabeth wanted to know how her friend had done it. How she'd survived without finding another to love.

Elizabeth walked through the doors, breathing in the scents of the Grand Hotel. The rich smell of polish that left the walnut wood gleaming. The mouthwatering smell of Mrs. Hall making bread for breakfast. The fresh flowers that appeared each and every day.

Scents that reminded her of being alive. She, Elizabeth Hamilton, was alive while her husband was dead. Steven's job on Earth was done, and now he sat among the Saints of Heaven. Her job had yet to be completed, and she'd better get to work and figure out what that was.

Lizzie-girl, live your life. I will always be near. Be the woman I knew you always were. The one I fell deeply in love with.

"Mrs. Hamilton?"

Elizabeth turned from Steven's voice to the one calling her name. Blinking several times, her gaze focused on the kind and gentle brown eyes of Auggie.

"Stewart, please get Mrs. Hamilton a glass of water," Auggie ordered, then his hand was upon her elbow, their gazes locked on each other.

"Elizabeth?" he whispered.

"Yes, I...I am fine," Elizabeth responded, her heart thumping behind her breast.

"Mr. Raines?" Stewart's concerned voice made her turn in his direction and smile.

"Mrs. Hamilton, please come to my office and sit for a moment. Stewart has brought you some water," Auggie kindly offered, his otherwise cheerful gaze marred with concern.

A swoosh of feeling grounded slammed into Elizabeth. She looked at Auggie again. For a moment, his eyes held something close to an emotion she'd not seen before. Then the flicker of emotion was gone.

Drawing in a deep breath, she straightened herself and turned toward the dining room.

"Mr. Raines, I have work that must be done today. If you wish to discuss anything with me, please do so there." Elizabeth strolled steadily through the dining room to her sewing room, her heart continuing its rapid beating. She could feel Auggie within inches behind her.

The door closed softly. She took her seat near the window, picking up the garment she'd started working on yesterday. A simple shirt in need of repairs in the seam and a tear in the sleeve as well as a few buttons to replace.

"Elizabeth, what happened back there?" Auggie asked. "You gave me cause to panic."

"I do apologize, Auggie." She threaded a needle then looked up at him. He knelt in front of her, close enough that she thought she could hear the rapid beat of his heart. "I'm not sure. It may have been the collective smells of the lobby that caught me off guard this morning."

"You are feeling better now then?" Auggie asked, concern for her still edging his words.

"Yes," she laughed. "I am not going to leave this Earth anytime soon, Auggie. At least not today.

"I'm sorry if I scared Stewart as well. It has been an unusual morning, and I'm afraid my mind was in another place. Many things have taken me by surprise in such a short time." Elizabeth placed the shirt in her lap, fighting the urge to reach out with a reassuring touch of her hand.

"Elizabeth, do you feel well enough to dine with me tonight?" Auggie asked suddenly, pacing the small room. "I know this may seem, well...I'm not sure what it seems." He nervously laughed.

"I don't think that would be appropriate, do you, Auggie?" Elizabeth looked away to hide she'd very much like to have dinner with him. The idea of sharing a meal with someone other than the dust in her house, or one of the other widows, excited her. Yet, would it just invoke more gossip about their relationship, or lack of?

"I understand your hesitation. If it's the issue of having a chaperone, would you that prefer Mrs. Hall or Mrs. Alexander join us?" Auggie suggested, stuffing his hands into his pant pockets.

"Why not both of them and make a dinner party out of it?" Elizabeth suggested, picking the shirt back up, not daring to look him in the face should her expression reveal too much. It was too soon for her to be entertaining the idea of dining alone with a man. Wasn't it? Another thing to discuss with Willa.

"Very well. Arrive with Mrs. Hall and Mrs. Alexander about six o'clock." Auggie snapped his fingers, a smile reflecting in his voice. "I'll make arrangements for dinner with both of them."

CHAPTER 9

Auggie could barely contain himself as he walked through the dining room, across the lobby, and into his office. Closing the door, he took a deep breath, smiling.

"She agreed! With conditions, of course, but Elizabeth agreed nonetheless." He hadn't felt this giddy since Jenny Smith went to the harvest school dance with him at twelve years old.

The stolen kiss behind the school. He'd felt so grownup—for about three seconds. That's when Jenny's older brother threw him to the ground by the shirt collar, warning him to stay away from Jenny. It had taken Auggie years before he ever thought of stealing kisses again.

And he had no intention of kissing Elizabeth Hamilton. He only wanted to have dinner with her. Get to know her. Possibly become her friend instead of only her employer.

That made him feel like that schoolboy. Having her around every day made him realize how lonely he was.

"Stewart!" Auggie called, knowing the desk clerk was within earshot. Stewart rarely left his post at the lobby desk.

"Yes, Mr. Raines?" Stewart stepped just inside the door and waited.

"Stewart, I'd like you to deliver a message to Mrs. Alexander for me." Auggie pulled out a notecard and pencil. "Come back in ten minutes to collect the note. While I'm writing it, please ask Sally to give my apartment an extra going over today. I'll be expecting guests for dinner tonight. Oh, and tell her there will be something extra in her pay this week for doing so."

"Yes, sir." Stewart nodded then left the room in a flurry.

That boy is always in a hurry to get somewhere, especially when it comes to Sally, Auggie thought, chuckling as his pencil scratched across the paper.

Willa,
I would be honored if you were to join Mrs. Hamilton, Mrs. Hall, and me for dinner tonight. I do hope to see you at 6:00 at the Grand.
Auggie

Auggie read over the note then folded it in half before placing it into an envelope. On the front, he quickly wrote "Mrs. Willa Alexander" and waited for Stewart to return.

Those few minutes gave him plenty of time to let a seed of doubt be planted in his mind.

What if dinner backfired and blew up in his face? What if Willa and Mary refused to accept his invitation. Worse yet, what if Elizabeth only saw him as her employer and not a potential friend?

Shaking his head, he sat back in the worn leather chair. It was comfortable, much like seeing Elizabeth each day had become comfortable. And the fit was just right. Perfect for him.

What am I thinking about? The blasted chair? Or Elizabeth?

Bolting out of the chair, he sent it crashing into the wall.

"She is *not* a piece of furniture, you fool!" he exclaimed, looking out the sole window in his office.

"Excuse me, Mr. Raines."

"Yes, Stewart?" He kept looking out the window, doing his best to get his emotions under control. To put them back into their hiding place before turning around.

"Sally is going to your apartment to give it an extra cleaning."

"Excellent." Auggie turned and nodded as he reached for the handwritten invitation.

"Please take this to Mrs. Alexander. I don't need to wait for a reply as I'm sure she'll arrive as requested," Auggie said, handing Stewart the envelope.

Taking the note, Stewart left Auggie to his own thoughts. *Now to get Mary to agree to making and eating dinner with us. How hard can that be?*

Auggie stepped out of his office, not at all surprised to find James behind the lobby desk covering for Stewart.

"James, I'll be in the kitchen should you need me for anything." Auggie walked quickly toward the back of the hotel. His steps slowed as he approached the kitchen door. Pausing for a moment, he listened to the cheerful singing. It had been awhile since he'd heard Mary singing. He rather liked it and wished she'd do it more often. She had a nice, soft, beautiful voice.

He cleared his throat as he stepped into the kitchen, almost laughing at the look on her face.

"Oh my!" Mary exclaimed after peeling herself off the ceiling. "I didn't hear you come in, Auggie."

"I didn't mean to frighten you." Auggie shuffled toward her, feeling like a boy who was about to tell a secret but afraid to do so. "I haven't heard you sing like that for a very long time."

"That's because you don't come into the kitchen like you used to," she said, turning her attention back to the stove. "You've stayed either in your office or your apartment, until lately, that is."

"I'm trying to change that." He laughed. "Mary, how do you feel about making a special dinner tonight for four?"

Turning away from the stove, Mary squinted at him. "What sort of dinner?"

"Nothing too special. Simple yet hearty." Auggie shuffled several items on the counter around, only to have her put them right back where they'd been.

"Humph! Spill it, Auggie, before you break something I can't mend."

Auggie drew in a breath of courage then

spewed out his words. "I would be honored if you would join Willa and I for dinner tonight at six."

"Why would you want to have dinner with two elderly women when— That's only three people, Auggie. Who is the fourth?"

Auggie looked up at her with a grin on his face. "Actually, there is a fourth for dinner. Elizabeth— er—Mrs. Hamilton has agreed to come as well."

"Oh, *Elizabeth*," Mary teased, turning back to mixing ingredients. "And whose idea was it to ask Willa and me to attend what could be an intimate dinner for two?"

"Mrs. Hamilton thought it would be inappropriate if we dined together in my private apartment alone," Auggie replied, rocking back on his heels, hands in his pockets.

"And so it would," Mary agreed.

"Since I agreed, I suggested you and Willa join us." Auggie was quite proud of himself for not pushing Elizabeth to dine without two very special matriarchs.

"Do you have a menu planned? Or are you going to eat whatever I have for our hotel guests?" Mary asked, hands on her hips and an expectant look on her face.

"No, I don't," Auggie admitted, then smiled. "I thought I would leave that in your capable hands. I don't know what your schedule is for tonight. Or what you have in the pantry."

"Simple and unassuming would be best," she said, flipping through her recipe box. "I may have something in mind that will work."

"Then you'll come?" Auggie asked, raising his

eyebrows, hoping she'd say she would be there.

"I wouldn't miss this for anything!" Mary laughed. "Now get out of here. I've work to do both in and out of this kitchen."

"Yes, ma'am." Auggie saluted, leaving his old confidant to her recipe box.

"MR. RAINES." ELIZABETH smiled, lowering her eyes slightly.

"Mrs. Hamilton." Auggie nodded with a slight bow. "I am looking forward to our dinner at six."

"I will remember to be prompt." Elizabeth smiled, feeling a flush of heat rise in her cheeks.

They both paused a moment longer, looking at each other before continuing on their individual journeys.

When Elizabeth reached the kitchen, she found Mrs. Hall mumbling and rummaging through a stack of recipes, tossing one after another aside.

"No, that won't do at all," Mary insisted, shoving aside yet another notecard. "Ah, here it is!"

"Can't decide on lunch, Mrs. Hall?" Elizabeth asked, holding back the giggle struggling to surface.

"What? No. Yes." Mary laughed. "It's for dinner tonight. It seems I will be dining with you and Auggie."

"Oh? That's good news," Elizabeth replied, touching her on the arm. "It won't be too much trouble for you, will it?"

"Not at all, my dear," Mary chirped, going over to the pantry.

"If you are sure, then I look forward to tonight." Elizabeth liked Mrs. Hall. She was like that doting aunt you love but don't get to see very often. "I wanted to ask if you wouldn't mind preparing an extra lunch plate on my tray. Mrs. Alexander will be joining me today."

"Umm, not at all, Mrs. Hamilton. I'll bring in the tray myself," Mary answered, scanning through the recipes once again.

"That won't be necessary. I can come and get it like any other day." Elizabeth began to insist further until she noticed Mrs. Hall was tapping her foot.

"Nonsense!" Mary insisted. "I haven't seen my dear friend for several weeks. It will give me an opportunity to at least say hello."

"All right." Elizabeth gave in, looking down to hide her smile. "Thank you, Mrs. Hall."

"Now, go on with you. I have a dinner to plan," Mary declared, turning back to the scattered recipes.

Lost in her thoughts, Elizabeth strolled through the hotel on her way back to her sewing room.

So, it would seem that she was having dinner with Auggie tonight. Mrs. Hall had agreed, but had Willa? If Willa declined, then she'd be free to go home to her sanctuary as they'd be missing one guest. Would she really cancel dinner if Willa decline Auggie's invitation to join them?

A wave of sadness swept over her. She didn't want to go back to an empty house. Yes, it was full of memories and the love she and Steven shared, but somehow *their* home had transformed into *her* home. Elizabeth wasn't quite sure how to handle that subtle and unexpected change.

Everything was changing without her taking notice. How and when did it all start? Her mind searched for answers while her heart wept with guilt.

Was there any harm if Auggie did become a friend? Would that mean she was betraying Steven's memory? His love?

Elizabeth picked up the cotton dress she'd been repairing for one of the hotel guests and inspected her work. Every stitch held the material together until it hadn't.

Much like her life as a happily married woman wildly in love with her husband had been held together. Their union had been stitched together tightly with their love until it blew apart several months ago. She blinked back the tears building in her eyes. Maybe the time for feeling sad had to stop. She must remember all their good times and their love—not feel sorry for herself that she'd been left alone. Because she wasn't alone. She had friends— old and new—to build a new life around.

Setting the garment onto her lap, Elizabeth wiped away the tears.

"I'll not be a victim of my own grief," she declared, threading the needle with a fresh strand of blue thread. "Even if Willa doesn't agree to attend, I'm still going to dinner. It won't hurt to have dinner with two new friends."

"Elizabeth?" Willa's voice followed behind the light knock upon the door.

Startled, Elizabeth pricked her finger. "Ouch! Willa, is it really time for lunch?" she asked, sucking the spot where the needle had stung her. "Been a long time since I stuck myself," she laughed, putting the mending away.

"No, not yet," Willa replied, taking a seat on the other side of the small worktable. "There is something I wish to discuss with you before then."

"Oh, there are a number of things I'd like to talk about with you as well," Elizabeth said, moving her sewing over onto the bench where several other items waited their turn at the needle and thread. "I just need to know—"

"Elizabeth, did you know about this?" Willa pulled an envelope from her skirt pocket, handing it to her.

"What's this?" Elizabeth turned the envelope over, immediately recognizing Auggie's handwriting. She burst out laughing. "Oh, Willa."

"Did you know about this invitation to dinner?" Willa asked, a concerned look on her face.

"Yes, I did." She stifled another round of giggling. "You must excuse me for finding this rather funny. Not only do I know about it, I informed Mr. Raines I wouldn't dine with him alone.

"He agreed and suggested asking both you and Mrs. Hall to join us. Are you agreeable to the arrangement?" Elizabeth waited for her friend to say she was. Not that it mattered anymore since she'd already made up her mind to have dinner with Auggie regardless.

The two friends continued discussing Elizabeth's newfound freedom in being able to provide for herself. What is was like working in the Grand. And how Elizabeth was happy to be able to stay on in Blessings Valley until a knock at the door startled both of them.

"Mrs. Hamilton?" Mrs. Hall's voice followed the tray that came through the opened door. "I have brought lunch for—oh! Hello, Willa."

"Oh! It's that time already?" Elizabeth asked surprised that the past few hours had flown by so quickly.

"Mary, you are looking well." Willa's gaze swept over Mrs. Hall and the tray she carried.

"As do you, Willa. It has been far too long since we last spoke." Mary set the tray on the table between Elizabeth and Willa, her gazed locked upon Willa.

"We must rectify that one day," Willa suggested as Mary nodded her agreement, a suspicious smile upon her face.

Elizabeth watched with amusement as the two exchanged one last look before Mrs. Hall walked out the door.

"What was that all about?" Elizabeth asked, spreading butter over a piece of bread. "I am not sure if it was friendly, or if I should call for staff to break up a potential fight."

"I'm not sure what you are concerned about. It was nothing, I suppose." Willa poured coffee into their cups, dropping a sugar cube into her own. "Now, what was it you wanted to discuss with me?"

Elizabeth put the bread down, adjusting the napkin on her lap. "I'm scared I am forgetting Steven," she confessed, the tears returning to her eyes.

"What do you mean?" Willa gushed, surprise in her voice.

"I'm starting to dread going home each night. It

is so quiet there. And the house feels, well, it feels cold and empty." Elizabeth let the tears creep down over her cheeks.

"Elizabeth, you'll never forget your husband or the life you shared with him." Willa reached over, covering Elizabeth's hand.

"Are you sure, Willa?" Elizabeth stood then turned toward her. "Look at me! This morning, I found myself putting on clothes that aren't suitable for a widow. Yet I did nothing to change them."

"Who says they aren't suitable? You look lovely, and the light is returning to your face," Willa noted, smiling softly at her. "You are starting to get on with your life, Elizabeth. There's nothing wrong with that."

"But—" Elizabeth began, then sank down into the chair. "Is it right they somehow make me feel alive again?"

"Steven wouldn't want you to spend the rest of your days mourning for him. He'd want you to go on and live the rest of your life in peace and happiness. Maybe even find love one day."

"I don't know if I could ever love another man the way I did Steven." Elizabeth wiped her nose. She was acting like a little girl, but she didn't care. It felt like she was losing sight of her best friend in life.

"Elizabeth, do you want to cancel dinner tonight?" Willa's words were edged with concern that matched the look in her eyes.

"No!" Elizabeth's heart skipped a beat at the thought of not seeing Auggie for dinner. "I mean, it would be disrespectful to do so. Mrs. Hall is planning something special. Auggie—I mean, Mr. Raines—agreed readily to my conditions to dine with him."

"I see," Willa said, smiling. "Do you find Mr. Raines…appealing?"

"Willa! I find Mr. Raines to be someone I'd like to consider a friend one day. He's been nothing but kind and honorable to me while I've been here," Elizabeth exclaimed, feeling her cheeks turn several shades of pink. She'd never thought of whether or not she was attracted to Auggie other than maybe as a friend. Certainly not as a romantic possibility! It was too soon for such notions, if she ever entertained those feelings again. Which she wouldn't.

"Then you have your answer." Willa placed a sandwich on her plate alongside a spoonful of fruit.

"Yes, I suppose I do." Elizabeth smiled, feeling some of the weight of guilt lift.

They continued eating and laughing about several things happening about town. How the boardinghouse would be receiving some new miners on the next train. Elizabeth told Willa about how she spent her days working at the Grand.

"Goodness, I really need to get back," Willa announced. "I'll take the tray back into the kitchen. It will give me a chance to speak with Mary again."

Elizabeth nodded. "Thank you for coming to lunch, Willa. And for agreeing to have dinner. You are a true friend and one I am honored to have in my life."

"My dear Elizabeth, you are like a daughter to me," Willa chimed, picking up the tray and leaving the room for the kitchen.

Elizabeth smiled. For the first time in months, her heart and soul felt lighter. And happier.

WALKING INTO THE kitchen where Mary was preparing a large piece of beef, Willa set the tray of soiled dishes on the counter and waited for her to acknowledge her presence.

"What do you propose, Willa?" Mary asked after several minutes, putting the pan into the icebox.

"We must find a way to get them together." Willa leaned over the counter. "Mary, don't you see how perfect they would be for each other?"

"I do," Mary turned toward Willa, wiping her hands down her apron. "But I'll not have two broken hearts on my shoulders! Auggie has suffered enough humiliation in his life. He came to Blessings Valley hoping to escape the ridicule of his unfortunate riding accident. He lives with the belief he'll only be loved for his massive fortune, not for the man I know him to be."

"Really, Mary, don't you think Elizabeth has been suffering as well?" Willa asked softly. "Or have you forgotten what it is like to have lost the love of your life?"

"Have you?" Mary asked, irritation flickering in her eyes. "We've been friends for many years. Must we quarrel over this?"

Willa let go of the breath she'd been holding, afraid she would have to bite her tongue. Then she realized they were both only concerned for the happiness of two young people they both admired and loved like they were their own children.

"Elizabeth is struggling as she starts to let go of her grief, and she's not a fortune hunter by any means. I have also noticed she turns a pretty shade of pink when she speaks of Auggie." Willa smiled, hoping Mary got her meaning.

"You know, now that you mention it, I have noticed that in her and in him as well. Auggie's eyes light up whenever he mentions Elizabeth," Mary replied, cutting more vegetables then opening the icebox and putting them in with the pan of beef. "Could it be their hearts are turning toward each other and they don't know it?"

"Isn't that the way of love, Mary?" Willa grinned. "It sneaks up on you, then hits you in the middle of your heart like a lightning bolt."

"Let's wait and see how dinner is before we do any meddling, shall we?" Mary suggested "Agreed?"

"Agreed!" Willa smiled.

AUGGIE PACED HIS apartment, pausing every few moments to check the time on his pocket watch. Why he was nervous about dinner escaped him. Granted, it had been quite some time since he'd had dinner guests. Was that the reason for feeling anxious or was he doubting his decision to ask Elizabeth to dine with him after work hours? And in his private residence?

"Fifteen minutes," he noted, pulling on the collar of his shirt to ease the uncomfortable tightness forming around his throat. "Why did I not think this through before plunging forward? The evening may end in disaster, and I can't have that."

The sound of the dumbwaiter drew his attention. Mary wouldn't be far behind, dressed for dinner. Too late to back out now.

He didn't want to, plain and simple. By all accounts, Elizabeth was anything but a woman looking to advance her current situation. Besides, no one other than himself, and Mary of course, knew his background and the size of the fortune he was to inherit. Not to mention what his assets in the hotel were.

His father owned a successful shipping enterprise. One that had kept Auggie in the best schools and surrounded by the best families. It had been expected that he would marry into high society, but he wanted to marry for love, not station or rank among his peers.

So, he'd gone and convinced his father a fortune could be made in the West. As Auggie always suspected, money meant more than family. His father agreed to give him a loan at the highest possible lending rate to build the hotel.

His father had told him he expected Auggie to return home before the end of the year, broke and thankful to be back in the comforts of wealth. That was a year ago. At least he'd earned his father's respect—finally.

"Auggie!" Mary's voice happily intruded upon his unpleasant memories.

"Coming, Mary," Auggie answered, making his way to the hallway.

"Would you please help me?" Mary stood beside the open dumbwaiter filled with various serving bowls and platters, as well as plates and silver.

Auggie smiled, stepping out of his apartment door. There wasn't much he wouldn't do for Mary for the rest of her days. Even if it meant carrying plates of food into his living space for his own dinner party.

"I believe you have done more than enough, Mary. I could have asked the entire town for dinner!" Auggie teased, picking up the large platter of braised beef and various vegetables. "It smells delicious. Are you trying to fatten me up?" He winked.

Mary laughed, a tray of glasses and a few bottles of wine in her hands. "You are not in need of fattening up, Auggie! What you are in need of is a companion every so often."

Carrying the platter into the apartment, Auggie set his on the table then relieved Mary of the tray she was carrying.

"That is a very old and tired subject, Mary. I take pleasure in your companionship, as well as my employees. All day. Every day," Auggie insisted with a crooked smile on his face, thinking of Elizabeth. "Why must you continue to treat me like a boy needing to be looked after?"

"Because, Auggie, there are times you need looking after," Mary scolded. "Now, please go get the rest of the food while I set the table. Your other guests will be here any minute."

"Yes, ma'am!" Auggie saluted, snapping his heels together.

He never expected a mother figure once he'd

become a man and struck out on his own. Little did Mary know he'd overheard his mother giving her strict instructions about looking after him. It was the only reason she'd had been allowed to come with him.

"My little secret," he whispered.

"What secret is that, Mr. Raines?"

Elizabeth's sweet voice sent waves of heat through him.

"Nothing of importance to anyone but me," Auggie answered, noting Elizabeth had arrived with Willa. "I'm pleased you could join us, Mrs. Alexander."

"Oh, I wasn't about to miss a dinner cooked by Mrs. Hall!" Willa chimed, smiling as she strolled into his apartment.

"Here, let me take something," Elizabeth offered, taking a plate of cups filled with pudding. "I think Mrs. Hall outdid herself today. I do hope it wasn't too taxing on her with her duties in the hotel dining room."

"If I know Mrs. Hall, she found it enjoyable." Auggie grabbed the bowl wrapped in a cloth. "I left the menu up to her. She hasn't been able to cook like this for a very long time, I'm afraid."

"Come, children, before everything gets cold!" Mary called from the doorway.

"We have been summoned." Auggie grinned, waiting as Elizabeth stepped lightly through the door ahead of him.

She'd changed into a rather attractive blue dress with a simple belt that fit her waist perfectly. Her auburn hair was piled elegantly upon her head with little curly strands escaping here and there. The only piece of jewelry was her wedding ring.

Auggie was sure Willa must have brought the dress and fixed Elizabeth's hair for her. He didn't remember seeing Elizabeth bring any extra items to work with her this morning.

Auggie placed the warm bowl on the table then stood at his chair, waiting for the chatting ladies to take their seats. Mary and Willa had already claimed seats next to each other, leaving Elizabeth no choice but to sit next to him.

He didn't mind. He would have preferred sitting across from Elizabeth so that he could look at her without being detected. Now every time he wanted a peek, he'd have to turn his head, letting everyone know his interest.

His attraction to Elizabeth would be revealed.

CHAPTER 10

Elizabeth shot Willa a look that could have put her six feet under. She was not pleased with the obvious meddling in her life. How many times must she tell Willa she had no interest in finding another man to marry. Or love for that matter.

And then to make sure she sat next to Auggie—well! That was pushing things a bit. And judging by the look on Mrs. Hall's face, Elizabeth surmised Willa had an accomplice. Looking at their faces, her anger slipped away. How could she remain upset with two kindly ladies who only meant well? Who cared enough about her well-being to meddle?

Glancing over at Auggie, her heart warmed. The smile on his face producing little smile lines at the corners of his eyes which softened an otherwise stoic appearance. The navy-blue suitcoat fit him perfectly. The white starched shirt with a very stiff collar a sharp contrast to the darkness of the jacket. He'd taken care, making sure his hair was combed in place, even going so far as to trim his beard, which she was sure he'd done this morning.

Elizabeth often wondered what lay beneath the facial hair. She imagined he had a strong, angular jaw with a dimpled chin. Maybe one day she'd have the chance to see for herself.

Listen to yourself! I have no business wondering anything about another man. Steven's body is barely gone from this Earth and I'm thinking how attractive Auggie is!

Yet she couldn't help but notice that here, in his private quarters, he was perfectly at ease and appeared happy. All the worries of the hotel were left at the apartment door. How could she not feel a small attraction to him?

"Mrs. Hamilton, would you care for some of the braised beef?" Auggie's simple question resulted in a blush of heat brushing her cheeks. She smiled then took a piece from the platter. "Ladies, may we dispense with formality tonight? I would much rather use first names since we are in my home."

"Yes, of course." They agreed in unison.

"Everything smells marvelous, Mary," Elizabeth complimented, spooning a few of the vegetables on her plate as well. "I do hope this didn't cause you any distress in preparing such a lavish meal. I'd hate to think you felt overworked in the kitchen preparing an extra meal just for tonight."

"Nonsense, Elizabeth. I haven't been asked to prepare a meal for an intimate party in quite some time. I rather enjoyed it," Mary gushed. "I do hope

Auggie will have another opportunity for more dinner guests in the future. He rarely leaves his work; often times falling asleep in his office chair. Don't you, Auggie?"

"Now, Mary, you know very well the hotel keeps me quite busy," Auggie protested, slicing into the beef. "If I didn't keep up on the running of things, we could all very well be out of jobs. I owe it to my employees to know they are well taken care of."

"How did you come by the hotel, Auggie?" Elizabeth had been wondering for the past few weeks what the process of obtaining a business was but felt it inappropriate to ask. Now that they were having dinner with Mary and Willa, she saw no reason not to ask.

"The same as any other businessman would, I suppose," Auggie replied vaguely, not making eye contact with anyone except Elizabeth. "You find a funding source and present your plans. With any luck, the representative will consider you a good investment. Once that happens, the loan for the requested funds is made and its terms presented."

Auggie smiled then shifted his gaze from her to Mary. It was that exchange between them that surprised her. Elizabeth may have been out of touch with the goings on in the everyday world these past months, but she certainly recognized the look of secrecy when she saw it.

Could it be Auggie was overextended on his finances? Was his loan being called in? Or was it something else entirely? Something from his past? She couldn't imagine him doing anything dishonest or dishonorable, ever. Elizabeth was sure she was wrong, and everything was perfectly alright with Auggie.

"Did you take out a bank loan or something else?" Elizabeth continued, curious as to the mystery of how one started a business. Especially when it was a woman who was inquiring to secure a loan. And being a penniless widow, Elizabeth thought she'd be a target for some unsavory man trying to exploit her situation for his own good. Not that she had much to exploit.

"Elizabeth!" Willa exclaimed as Mary coughed and Auggie burst out laughing. "Those are highly personal questions."

"Mrs. Hamilton—err—Elizabeth, are you thinking of putting me out of business one day soon?" Auggie asked, his eyes dancing with humor as he sat back in the chair.

Elizabeth dabbed the corner of her mouth then placed the napkin back on her lap smiling. Had she really given him that impression? She'd asked a simple question really. Not unusual as far as she was concerned.

"By no means at all. Between Willa's boardinghouse and the Grand, I don't believe Blessings Valley has room for another lodging establishment," Elizabeth replied, her eyes meeting the astonished ones of both Willa and Mary. "I am only curious. Now that I am on my own, I have been thinking of my own future. One day, I may want to open a dress shop. I was inquiring as to how to obtain financial backing to do so."

Her gaze swept back to Auggie, the smile on

his face soothing her fear she'd offended him. If anything, he looked pleased of her proclamation to make something of herself without anyone's help. Well, outside of a loan, that was.

"You should have asked me, Elizabeth," Willa stated, harshness edging her words. "I would have given you advice. Maybe even invested in your shop."

Elizabeth looked at Willa, cringing at her expression.

"Yes, Willa, I could have. But I know how you were able to fund your boardinghouse," Elizabeth said, folding her napkin on her plate. How was she going to let her friend know that she didn't want to risk their friendship over a business matter? "Unfortunately, Steven didn't leave me with that kind of money. I have been left to my own wits and must find my way, Willa. Make a life for myself. So you see why I may want to know how Auggie started out, don't you?"

"It's a reasonable enough question," Auggie said, reaching for her hand.

His warm touch radiated through her, sending shivers to places once meant for her husband. She withdrew from him, folding her hands securely in her lap.

"I secured a loan from a, ah, friend of the family." Auggie poured some wine for them all before making eye contact with Mary for a moment or two. "He thought the idea of a hotel in the West was intriguing but needed more information. And he'd have a place to stay should he ever venture this way, which is highly unlikely. It wasn't easy though. It took a lot of planning and convincing him I was a good investment after all."

He's hiding something, Elizabeth thought, suddenly feeling foolish and uncomfortable. *Something that he wishes to remain secret. Does Mary know, I wonder?*

"Well, I have had quite enough business talk." Willa stood, gathering dishes one by one. "It's still fairly early, and I would like to hear a bit of music. Do you have a gramophone, Auggie?"

"I do, Willa." Auggie smiled. "I even have several recordings."

"Wonderful, something to dance to would be nice," Willa suggested, looking over at Elizabeth.

No, Elizabeth mouthed, shaking her head. She was not about to dance with her boss, even with two chaperones in the room.

Auggie crossed the room and rummaged through his recordings until he found one. Preparing the gramophone, a Sousa's Band recording started, and he headed back to the table.

"Mrs. Hamilton, may I have this dance?" he asked, offering a hand for her to accept.

Elizabeth stared at his extended hand, her breath caught in her throat. Without another thought, she placed her hand in his, allowing him to guide her to the center of the room. His arm slipped around her waist, and he guided her with expertise to the melody of *Phroso* waltzes.

The room around them melted away. There was just him and her. No one from the outside world to give their opinion. Only the two of them and the music.

The music stopped, and they stood in the middle of room. Auggie held her in his arms, gazing down on her. Elizabeth felt her breath catch in her throat for a moment.

She had to get out of there. This wasn't right. She belonged to Steven.

She shouldn't be in the arms of Auggie Raines, plain and simple.

"You work on Elizabeth, and I'll do the same with Auggie. These kids need a push, and I'm not afraid to give him one right in the middle of his back!"

Somewhere in the dreamy fog she thought she heard talking but couldn't be sure she'd heard correctly.

DUSK BEGAN TO fully claim the night as Auggie walked through the street with Elizabeth and Willa. They strolled in quiet comfort the short distance from the hotel to the boardinghouse, each of them lost in their own thoughts.

Auggie felt a spring in his step. It had been far too long since he'd enjoyed a night like this one. Dancing with Elizabeth reminded him of those days—and nights—spent at debutante events. The joy of music shared with an attractive woman in his arms.

He even quite enjoyed taking a turn around the room with Mary and Willa. They reminded him of one of his elderly widowed aunts.

But it was Elizabeth who had made him feel alive with hope again. Hope that maybe he could one day find love with the right woman. Could that woman be Elizabeth? It was too soon to tell, but it was a good start in finding out.

"Thank you for joining us tonight, Willa," Auggie said as they approached the boardinghouse. "I really enjoyed the evening. Especially dancing with two special women several times."

"It has been a long time. I'm not sure you enjoyed it as much as Mary and I did however." Willa laughed, stopping at her porch stoop.

"On the contrary, it was quite enjoyable," Auggie insisted, "regardless of who my dancing partner was."

"Humph!" Willa exclaimed, a smile on her face. "At least your feet were spared. Alas, the night has ended, and I must get some rest for there are several boarders expected tomorrow. Thank you for inviting me as I did enjoy myself. It was good to spend a few hours with Mary, as well.

"Elizabeth, you are welcome to stay the night if you prefer not walking home tonight," Willa offered as she walked up the steps. "I would rather you not travel the path home this close to nightfall alone."

"She won't be alone, Willa," Auggie said, offering his elbow to Elizabeth, only to withdraw it when she refused.

Blast! Nothing has changed between us. And here I thought that maybe it had.

"Auggie has offered to accompany me, and I would much rather sleep in my own bed tonight," Elizabeth answered, taking a step away from him.

Auggie had hoped after their evening together Elizabeth would have changed her mind about him. Had he offended her in some way? He didn't think so. Yet, she still wouldn't yield to him being a gentleman.

"I will make sure she arrives safe and sound on her doorstep, Willa." Auggie smiled, looking from Willa back to Elizabeth. "I give my word as a gentleman."

"Well, since it has all been arranged, then I shall say goodnight." Willa turned and walked into her boardinghouse.

Once lights were on, Auggie and Elizabeth continued on the path toward the row houses provided by the mining company where she and the other widows still lived.

"Did you enjoy yourself tonight, Elizabeth?" Auggie clasped his hands behind his back to keep from touching her in any way.

"Yes, I did. Thank you for inviting me," Elizabeth replied, her gaze on the path straight ahead of them. "Mary prepared a fabulous meal, don't you agree? I believe it is the best I've ever had. You are lucky to have her under your employment at the hotel."

"I am pleased you had a good time." Auggie smiled, pride washing over him. He had hoped she enjoyed his company and dancing with him after all she'd gone through these past months. It had to be devastating to have lost someone you pledged to love forever. "As for Mary, I am extremely blessed to have her."

"How did you ever find her? Someone of her skills should be running a kitchen in a big fancy house somewhere, not in a small hotel in the West," Elizabeth remarked, looking over at him, her expression lost in the rays of the setting sun. "I am only curious and don't mean to pry."

"You aren't. And you are correct, of course. Mary did run a kitchen in a big house once for many years." Auggie began weighing his next words carefully. He wasn't prepared to reveal how well he knew her, not yet anyway. "She is an old friend of my family. When she heard of my venture, she all but told me that the kitchen would be hers. And as you can imagine, she's hard to say no to."

"That is an understatement." Elizabeth laughed, her gaze settling on his for several moments for the first time since they'd left the Grand.

He could never get enough of looking into her kind blue eyes. Elizabeth was the sweetest and strongest woman of her age he'd ever had the privilege to come to know. The fact that she didn't fully realize that strength impressed him all the more.

"I much admire that in a woman," Auggie said, deciding to test the waters with some personal frankness. "It is one of the reasons I knew I had to bring you on as a seamstress."

"You don't say?" Elizabeth asked, surprised by his confession. "I thought I was a little pushy and sounded a tad desperate, I'm afraid. I all but pleaded with you to hire me, or don't you recall?"

"On the contrary." Auggie took her elbow and stopped walking. "You are intelligent, resourceful, and determined. Not to mention driven, even if you don't realize it. These are all qualities I look for in a woman. I mean an employee."

"I never thought of myself in those terms,"

Elizabeth replied, the night sky reflecting in her eyes.

Her lips, as well as her flawless face, were free of any makeup. He hadn't noticed it before, but tonight it felt like everything was becoming clearer to him. As if he were seeing her for the very first time.

"Elizabeth," he said, pulling her to him. They stared into each other's eyes, their bodies very close. Auggie moved to steal a kiss when the church bell announced the hour.

Elizabeth's eyes widened in astonishment. "Oh, um, forgive me…"

"No, it is I who must ask for forgiveness. I lost my head for a moment," Auggie begged, feeling like the heel he was sure she saw standing before her.

"I live just over there." She pointed, stepping away from him and quickly walked toward the porch.

"I promised to see you home and I shall," Auggie proclaimed, stepping up beside her. Those few steps felt like miles widened by the uncomfortable silence between them.

"This is home," Elizabeth said, stepping upon her porch.

"Then I shall say goodnight, but first I must thank you for a very pleasant evening. It was an honor to have you as my guest for dinner." Auggie smiled, bowing slightly. "I'll see you in the morning?"

"It was a very pleasant occasion, Auggie. Goodnight." Elizabeth opened her door then turned back toward him, a smile playing on her lips. "See you in the morning."

Auggie smiled, nodded, then turned back toward town once he was certain Elizabeth was safely in her home. He felt like he'd just won the Kentucky Derby.

ELIZABETH CLOSED THE door then lit a lamp on one of the tables. She waited a few minutes then peeked out a window to see if Auggie had gone.

The disappointment to find that he had left took her by surprise. What had she expected? That he would be waiting for her to open the door and—and what? Why was everything in her world tilting again? Would the constant wave of emotion ever end?

Checking the door, making sure it was secure for the night, Elizabeth took the lamp and went up to her room. She suddenly longed to be out of the dress and in comfortable clothes now that she was finally home. Carefully removing the garment Willa graciously had loaned her, Elizabeth draped it across the back of a chair.

She never would have chosen one this beautiful shade of blue. Willa knew it too, which was why she'd insisted on choosing the perfect dinner dress and not giving Elizabeth any choice. If she'd been given the option, she would have chosen to attend dinner in the dress she'd put on at six this morning.

Pulling her nightgown down over her head and letting it fall freely over her, she reached for her robe. Wrapped snug in its familiar warmth, Elizabeth let her hair down and began stroking the long strands with the silver brush she'd received from Steven last Christmas. She ran a fingertip over the embossed roses, remembering how proud Steven was to have been able to give her such a beautiful gift.

"I'm sorry, Steven," she whispered, tears streaming down her face. "I have dishonored your memory, our marriage vows, and done the most sinful thing. I danced with another man! A man who is my employer. I fear he sees more than there is for me to give.

"I made a promise to love you and only you forever. I will keep that promise, but it felt nice to dance. To let the sadness of your death evaporate for a short time.

"Forgive me, my love."

Elizabeth turned out the bedroom lamp, laid her robe at the foot of the bed, and crawled under the handmade quilt. The bed once made for two now felt far too big for one. Hugging Steven's pillow, she continued to cry.

The guilt burned her deeply. How could she find enjoyment in the arms of another man?

Her marriage vows broken and for what? To feel alive for a few hours while her husband lay in a box surrounded by the cold, dark ground?

Elizabeth, he is a good man. You must not feel ashamed. I would not want you to live the rest of your life alone.

"But I have betrayed you and our love, Steven."

No, you haven't. Don't ever think that because you have started to move on with your life that you have betrayed me.

"I made a promise to you before God. I promised to love you and only you until death—"

Us do part. And we have parted for now, my love. When it is time for you to join me, I will be there to take your hand in mine.

"How can you be so sure?"

Trust in your faith and in God. He will never fail you, I promise.

"I will try, Steven. That's all I can do. I don't know if I'll ever really love another. You had my heart and soul, I couldn't give what's left to someone else."

When the time comes, you will know. You must open your heart to the possibilities.

Wiping the tears from her eyes, Elizabeth rolled over onto her back. Staring up into the darkness, her mind replayed the evening at Auggie's apartment.

She had enjoyed herself, that was true enough. And despite herself, she did find Auggie Raines an attractive man in many ways.

He was kind and considerate to his employees. He was obviously very fond of Mary as well. He had been light on his feet as he expertly guided her across the floor of his apartment. For those few moments, her heart felt light.

"And he hired a grieving widow to help her survive," Elizabeth whispered, hugging the pillow tighter to her chest. "What kind of person does that? I can't imagine any other reason for his kindness.

"He said I was strong, but am I really? Am I strong enough to one day give my heart to another?"

The chords of the waltz played through her mind. Humming the melody, she closed her eyes reliving those moments in Auggie's arms. When the world had disappeared, it was just the two of them. Holding each other. Gazing into each other's eyes as if they were two people in love.

How realistic could that be? The poor, grieving widow and the hotel owner seemed an unlikely match.

Unlikely, but not impossible if she'd open her heart once more to the possibility of love.

CHAPTER 11

Auggie woke in the wingback chair he'd fallen asleep in the previous night. His neck had a crick in it, and his once perfectly pressed dress shirt was now badly wrinkled.

Placing his glasses on the table, he ran his hands over his face. "Good grief," he yawned, stretching out cramped limbs. Pulling out his pocket watch, he groaned at the time. "Seven. I should be downstairs by now."

Pushing out of the chair, he shuffled into his bedroom stifling yet another yawn. Splashing water on his face from the wash basin, he met his mirrored gaze, shocked by how harried he appeared.

His hair was plastered on one side of his head while the other sprouted several rooster tails. He looked like he'd spent last night somewhere other than in his own home.

If he didn't know better, he'd think he'd spent the night with a bottle of whiskey and visions of

Elizabeth. What was it about her that had him in knots after dining together only once?

By no means had it been the intimate dinner for two he'd at first hoped for where they could get to know each other. It had been a quiet, uneventful evening with two widows acting as chaperones. Dancing with Elizabeth had been the highlight of the evening, seconded by seeing her safely to her front door. She had still refused a proper escort when he offered his arm. He must remember she was an independent woman now, showing the entire world there was no need for her to depend on a man any longer.

Elizabeth Hamilton was easygoing and quite pleasant to have a conversation with, even if it was only in regard to the work she was doing. Her beauty was most certainly more than skin-deep. It filled her entire being, as far as he could tell.

Up until last night when he saw her to the row houses on the edge of town, he'd only been in her company here at the hotel. And that was strictly business. Last night, however, wasn't. Now he wasn't sure what type of relationship they had, and whether or not it had changed.

He didn't want it to change—or did he? No, he quickly decided. He did not want it to change in the manner that she would leave his employment.

Would she keep a wide berth of him? Or would their day go on the same as always? Friendly and professional.

How was he going to learn more about her if everything has changed? Dinner certainly hadn't offered the opportunity, so how would working downstairs together do it?

Picking up his shaving soap, cup, and brush, he studied his beard closely.

What if he shaved it off? Would she only see the ugliness of the disfiguring scar? Would she cringe, walk away, and avoid him at all costs? Not willing to chance it, he put the brush back in the bowl. Auggie dried his face, rubbed his damp hair with the hand towel, then changed into a fresh shirt.

Knock knock.

"What kind of catastrophe has happened already this morning?" he wondered, finishing buttoning his shirt as he ambled out of the bedroom and across the floor "Yes, I'll be right there," he called out quickly, slipping into a suitcoat.

Answering the door, he was surprised to find Mary at the threshold, carrying a breakfast tray. "Mary, is everything all right?"

"It won't be if you stand there staring and you don't take this tray from me," she replied, waiting for him to take the tray. "Did you get Elizabeth home safely last night?"

"My apologies. I did, and you might as well sit down if you plan on putting me on trial." He relieved her of the serving tray, his stomach rumbling at the aroma of breakfast. Or was it revolting over what he was sure to come—Mary grilling him about Elizabeth.

"I have no idea what you mean, Mr. Raines," Mary feigned as she pressed past him and settled onto the settee. "But since you have invited me to stay, I see no point in not accepting."

Auggie shook his head, placing the tray on the

table where he'd had dinner with Elizabeth last night. What would it be like to share a private morning with her? Even though they'd eaten together many times in the hotel, here in his private quarters was something else altogether.

Intimate.

He could only imagine her buttering a plate of flapjacks, pouring maple syrup over them then licking her fingers free of any of the sticky syrup. He'd kiss away a spot she'd missed on the palm of her hand. She'd smile up at him, her eyes filled with—

"Auggie! Stop your daydreaming and come sit down," Mary strongly suggested, patting the spot next to her.

"So, I'm to be interrogated while sitting next to you?" Auggie teased, his vision evaporating as he turned around. "I'd much rather sit where I can anticipate your questions and look you in the face," he said, sitting back in the chair he'd slept in last night.

"As you please." Mary pinched her lips. "I'll not mince words. What do you plan to do about Elizabeth?"

His heart ceased to beat. Blood drummed in his ears.

"I'm not sure what you mean. Has she done something I'm not aware of?"

"No, because I am quite sure you are well aware of what she has done," Mary stated, sitting straighter.

Auggie glanced down at his clasped hands, his knuckles turning white. After all this time, had he misjudged Elizabeth? He couldn't think of one thing she might have done to offend Mary.

"Mary, what has happened between last night and this morning? As you well know, I am running a bit late and haven't been downstairs yet," Auggie said, breathing deeply to calm the rush of blood burning through his veins.

Mary looked over at him as if he'd lost his senses. "I hope a number of things have happened, if you are paying attention."

Auggie shook his head, tapped his fingers on the arm of the chair. "Please, Mary, do get to the point. I have never been good at riddles, as you well know."

"All right then, I shall." Mary shifted on the settee then fixed her gaze on him, sending a shiver through his body. "You are falling in love with Elizabeth, and I want to know what you plan to do about it!"

ELIZABETH SAT IN a front church pew, head bowed and hands clasped. She'd been here since shortly after waking this morning praying for forgiveness in dancing with a man she wasn't married to.

But it was more than that. Much more.

"Elizabeth, what are you doing here?" Fannie asked, a feather duster in her hand and brows furrowed with concern. "I haven't seen you in church for several weeks, except when you are scurrying by, to and from Blessings Valley."

"Asking for forgiveness, Fannie." Elizabeth look up at her friend through blurred vision. "I've sinned."

"You?" Fannie asked, astonished as she sat next to her. "Elizabeth, you are the last person I would ever think would sin on purpose. What do you think you have done to ask for God's forgiveness?"

"I danced with Mr. Raines last night. I allowed him to hold me close enough to feel his heart beating." Elizabeth felt the blush of shame sweep over her cheeks. "The worst of it is I...I enjoyed it."

"There is nothing wrong with dancing. Mr. Raines is an attractive man, as well as kind, from what I've heard. Everyone speaks fondly of him," Fannie said soothingly as if she were speaking to a frightened child.

Elizabeth cast her a glance then looked quickly away as tears filled her eyes. "I didn't think of Steven once while in Auggie's arms. I felt like a girl, not a married woman."

She felt Fannie's hands slip around hers, forcing Elizabeth to look into her face.

"You aren't married any longer. None of us are in the eyes of the law. We are widows. The rings we wear are symbols of the love we shared with our husbands. The memories are reminders of all we shared."

"You're wrong!" Elizabeth glared at Fannie, the tears streaming over her cheeks. "That may be true for you and the others, but not for me. I am a married woman."

She rose then all but ran out of the church, leaving Fannie behind in the pew. In Elizabeth's heart of hearts, she might believe Fannie was right, but she wasn't going to ever accept the truth of the matter.

She half-walked, half-ran along the path into town, her mind racing for reasons unclear to her. She couldn't focus on where she was going. Not until she found herself pounding on the door of the boardinghouse.

"Willa!" she cried out, wiping her tears with the back of her hand. When no answer came, she banged louder on the door. Of all the days for Willa not to be up early, it had to be today.

"Please answer the door," Elizabeth pleaded, her head bowed as she worried her hands. "Willa, where are you?"

After what seemed like hours instead of mere minutes, the door flew open.

"What is so urgent that—" Willa's eyes were wide with anger then worry. "Elizabeth, what is it? What has happened?"

"I am no better than a harlot, Willa!" she exclaimed, feeling the words spoken were as true as the sun rising this morning. She'd cheated on her deceased husband, plain and simple.

"Come inside before the entire town hears you." Willa held the door open, glancing up and down the street. "Let's go to the kitchen, I have a fresh pot of coffee on the stove and muffins ready to come out of the oven."

Elizabeth headed straight for the kitchen, taking a seat at the table. As she waited for Willa, she began to wonder if Fannie was right. Was she only having wishful thoughts of still being married to Steven? If she wasn't, then it would change everything her heart held so precious.

A once in a lifetime kind of love she's shared with Steven.

"So, what is this all about?" Willa asked as she took two cups from the cupboard. "I haven't seen you this upset since—"

"Go ahead, say it," Elizabeth said, tears leaving a trail down her cheeks. "Since Steven died."

"Yes, since Steven's death." Willa poured each of them steaming coffee then put the pot back on the stove before pulling the muffins from the oven. "What has happened since last night? You seemed so happy. I thought you were enjoying yourself so much that—"

"That's the problem." Elizabeth interrupted, not wanting to hear a word about the wonderful night she'd had. "I betrayed Steven by being in the arms of another man. And the worse part of it is that I did have a pleasant time. Then I got home, and the guilt drove into my soul, burning me with shame."

"My dear Elizabeth. There is no shame in finding joy. Steven wouldn't want you to live the rest of your life in a veil of black. He'd want you to go on facing each day as a gift. A gift of living and breathing. Of feeling the warmth of the sun. Smelling the freshness of the rain on a spring day." Willa looked at her with nothing but compassion. "Even find solace in the arms of another man. A good man who will treat you as good, or better, than Steven had."

"Then why haven't you found love, Willa? Why haven't you found someone as good as your late husband was?" Elizabeth asked, knowing full well it wasn't by Willa's choice. "I'm sorry. I shouldn't bring up the past where I have no business being."

"Be that as it may, if there comes a time that my heart finds love again, I'll marry." Willa stood, turning her back on Elizabeth. "Do you find Auggie Raines to be a good man?"

Elizabeth thought for a moment. Auggie Raines was a kind man to everyone at the hotel and to those in Blessings Valley as a whole. Would he be the same with a woman he cared for? Maybe even loved?

"Yes, I think so. He treats everyone that he encounters as an equal, especially those who work for him at the hotel," Elizabeth replied, wiping the tears from her face. "He has certainly shown me nothing but kindness. I find that most appealing."

Willa turned, a gentle smile on her face. "Then that is a start, Elizabeth. Follow your heart to the living. To someone who will love you as you deserve to be loved."

"But what if—" Elizabeth began.

"You'll have to find out for yourself. Now, I have to start breakfast." Willa put their cups into the sink.

"Thank you, Willa. I'm sorry I disrupted your morning with my foolishness." Elizabeth smiled, hugged her friend, then set out for the hotel.

"Today is a fresh start and a new life," she whispered, covering the distance between the boardinghouse and hotel with a new purpose. And a sense of peace.

FALLING IN LOVE with Elizabeth Hamilton? How

utterly ridiculous. They were as different as night and day. He was sure it would start with their backgrounds even though he didn't know much about Elizabeth. Other than she had been a seamstress before she'd married, then they'd come here to Blessings Valley for her husband to work in the mines.

That was a much as Auggie knew of her past.

What he knew about her this very day was she worked hard. Was a kind and generous woman to all those around her, including himself. On the rare occasion she was free of repair jobs, she would help out around the hotel whether it was mending a torn tablecloth or sewing on a button.

The present is what mattered, not the past. Hers nor his.

Pushing away from his desk, Auggie stepped out into the lobby. He had a mountain of work to do yet all he could think about was Elizabeth.

"Has Mrs. Hamilton arrived yet this morning?" he asked, walking over to the front doors and peering out the window.

"Yes, about fifteen minutes ago," Stewart replied. "Mrs. Hall hasn't brought her a breakfast tray yet."

"She hasn't?" Surprised, Auggie recognized an opportunity when one was laid right in front of him. "Well then, I shall go and get one for Mrs. Hamilton. It will save Mrs. Hall some time."

"As you wish, Mr. Raines," Stewart agreed, a small grin on his face.

Auggie gave him a side glance as he passed the front desk and then walked quietly to the kitchen.

With any luck, the tray would already be prepared and he wouldn't have to spend much time with Mary. He did not want another session of questioning like earlier this morning.

"I'm here to take Elizabeth her breakfast," he announced, walking into the kitchen.

"It's about time," Mary replied over a pan of sizzling bacon. "It's right there on the table."

"Thank you, Mary." Auggie went to pick up the tray noticing there was a place setting for two.

"You didn't eat earlier, now you can," Mary said, sliding the bacon onto a plate next to some flapjacks. "Take the small coffee pot with you."

"Yes, ma'am." Auggie plucked the pot off the stove, placing it on the tray then exited the kitchen unscathed.

Humph! I guess she said everything she wanted to, he thought, strolling through the hotel to the sewing room.

Standing at the slightly ajar door, a sweet humming came from within. A lovely tune that stirred his heart with joy.

"Elizabeth?" he called when the humming stopped, followed by the rustling of material.

"Come in," she answered.

Pushing open the door with a foot, he stopped short of entering. The sight of Elizabeth took his breath away. Usually neat as a pin, she looked as disheveled as he had been not long ago.

"Is everything alright?" he asked, concerned that she'd become ill overnight.

"Yes, it is now." She smiled up at him, her tired eyes red and swollen.

Auggie put the tray down and looked at her again. Shadows under her eyes spoke volumes.

"You didn't sleep well either, I take it," he remarked, pouring them each coffee. Had she been crying? How would he find out if she had been and why?

"Not really. Not at all," she confessed, gripping the item on her lap and avoiding making eye contact with him.

"Neither did I. In fact, I woke to find myself sitting in a chair. Mary's special coffee will wake us both up, I should think," he said, placing a cup of steaming brew in front of her. "I hope you were more comfortable than I was, at least. That chair may be comfortable enough for sitting in, but it lacks any of it as a substitute for a restful night in a bed."

His heart melted when Elizabeth looked up at him. Even a bit weary for the wear, she was beautiful. Behind the smile and tired eyes was a woman warring with herself.

Was last night the cause of it? Or had something happened since he left her on her porch stoop?

"Elizabeth, are you sure you're all right?" he asked, clasping his hands together to keep from taking her in his arms to sooth her. He wanted to chase away whatever was the cause of her sorrow.

"Yes, I think so," she answered, watching him. "Thank you for a lovely evening last night. I don't remember if I told you that or not."

Is that what is troubling her? Not being a gracious guest?

135

"It was a pleasure, Elizabeth. It has been quite some time since I dined with anyone." Auggie smiled, drinking the now warm black coffee. "Sadly, it reminded me how much I stay to myself these days."

"It was a pleasure, and that's what I have been struggling with." Tears glimmered in Elizabeth's eyes as her gaze swept across his face. "Steven has been gone for what seems only a short time, as if it were just yesterday when in reality it has been many months. He was the last man I danced with. The last man I took supper with. The last man I gave my heart to."

"And you miss him." Auggie suddenly understood what was upsetting her. It was more than just missing her husband. It was that fact that she'd had dinner with another man, namely him.

"Yes. I think I always will in some way." Elizabeth wiped away the tear, then shyly smiled. "Last night reminded me that I am alive, and at the same time, I felt guilty because of it. It reminded me what I have been missing by hoping for the impossible. That I'll go home one day and find Steven waiting for me. That death has not cheated me out of being married to a wonderful man."

Auggie could only nod. Even though he didn't fully understand the depth of her feelings, he could see it in her face. The love she had for her husband who could no longer return that love. The harsh reality of never having that love again must be devastating for her, and the other widows as well.

"My heart says I'm a married woman while my common sense quietly says otherwise. I am having difficulty accepting anything else."

Auggie gave up his handkerchief as tears washed down her face. His constant concern about his scar was completely unwarranted compared to the barrage of feelings he lay witness to on her face and in her eyes.

The sorrow.

The fear of uncertainty.

"I won't pretend to understand, Elizabeth. It pains me to see you in such agonizing turmoil." Hoping to draw her thoughts elsewhere, Auggie uncovered the serving dish to find bacon, eggs, and fried potatoes. "Are you by chance hungry? Mary will be on the warpath if this is not eaten."

"Yes, I suppose you are right." Elizabeth sighed lightly. "And now that you mention it, I am famished."

"Good. I have one more question to ask you." Auggie held his breath for a moment, then let it out. If his timing was off, so be it. But he didn't think the opportunity would come again any time soon. "Do you think there is a chance you might dine with me again sometime?"

The world came to a standstill as he waited anxiously for her answer. Had he moved to quickly? Her gaze bore right through to his soul. What was she looking for?

"Are you a good man, Auggie? An honest man?" Elizabeth sat back in the chair.

Her questions surprised him. Didn't she know him by now? Did she really think otherwise?

"I'd like to think so, Elizabeth."

"Then yes, I'll have dinner with you under one

condition," she said.

"What might that be?" Auggie hoped it would not be another night of four at the dinner table.

"That we go to Millie's Café. No more dining in your apartment," she said.

Auggie smiled, relief flooding through him. Could his loveless life be turning around?

"Agreed!"

CHAPTER 12

Several Days Later

"I'm going to dinner, not a dance, Willa!" Elizabeth said, exasperated by all the fussing about. Willa had been twisting her hair in every way possible for the past twenty minutes.

"A first public dinner is important. It shows your suitor how lovely you look when you step out for the evening," Willa explained as she continued to manipulate Elizabeth's hair to bend to her will.

"Auggie sees me every day. I am pretty sure he knows what I look like," Elizabeth remarked. "I see no practical reason to change my daily appearance. I don't want him to think I'm trying to snare him."

"I know he does. This is a different Elizabeth from the workplace. Have you forgotten what it is like to be courted?" Willa teasingly questioned. "He won't think anything that isn't already on his mind."

"Courted? Have you lost your senses?" Elizabeth turned to look at Willa only to have her head placed back in position.

"Keep your head straight and stop moving around," Willa instructed as she continued to twist and poke. "What would you call it then if it's not courting? Because from where I stand when a gentleman takes a lady out for dinner it is most definitely courting."

Elizabeth drew in a breath. "Friends spending time together. Auggie and I are friends. We most certainly are *not* courting, do you understand? Auggie has his business to take care of. It's far too soon for me to even consider if I want to be courted by Auggie, let alone any other man."

"Believe what you must," Willa laughed patting her on the shoulder. "There, I think I have finished. If I do say so myself, you look transformed into someone I don't recognize. Do you want to see for yourself?"

Did she? Part of her wanted to look while another part said it was wrong. Wrong in that she didn't want to see the old her give way to the new. She sucked in her bottom lip, threw caution to the wind, and nodded her head.

"Yes, I want to see." Elizabeth held her breath as she took the pewter hand mirror Willa handed her from behind. Laying it in her lap, she gazed down at the scrolled heart design on the back. It had been a gift from Steven one Christmas. Smiling at the memory, she closed her eyes and lifted the mirror.

"Go ahead, Elizabeth. There is nothing to fear,"

Willa whispered in her ear.

Slowly, she opened her eyes and gasped at the image of the stranger looking back at her. Her auburn hair was pulled up in a bun on a pillow of soft and fluffy hair. Ringlets and tendrils frame her face. She looked, and felt, years younger.

"Do you approve?" Willa asked.

"I haven't looked like this since—for some time now," Elizabeth said, her words soft and wispy. "Thank you, Willa."

"I hope you don't mind that I rummaged through your wardrobe and decided you should wear this." Willa smiled, holding up a light blue two-piece set. "If found it hidden away in a corner."

"I don't know, Willa. Is it too soon for something like this?" Elizabeth worried if the garment was too colorful for a widow. Yet she longed to put it on, just to see if she remembered how it felt on.

"No, it's not. Try it on and see before you decide to wear it or not," Willa suggested, holding out the skirt.

"Would you help me?" Elizabeth asked.

"I'd be honored." Willa held the skirt open.

Elizabeth stepped into the full deep pleated skirt then allowed Willa to fasten the back of it once the seams were straight. When she slipped into the long-sleeved stripped shirtwaist, she felt refreshed.

Willa buttoned up the lace bib yoke with no problems. One would think the fit was tailor made for Elizabeth, it fit that well in all the right places, and they'd be right. It was one of her own creations before she married Steven.

"Are you sure this isn't too much for Millie's?" Elizabeth hoped the answer was no. She couldn't help it but it felt quite comfortable against her body. And not one ounce of guilt was in her heart.

"Nonsense!" Willa insisted looking her over, checking to make sure everything was fastened and all the seams were straight. "A piece of jewelry would make it complete. Do you have anything?"

"Yes, I believe I do. A cameo my mother gave me. I'll go get it." Elizabeth ran up the stairs to her bedroom. Reaching her bureau, she opened the jewelry box, withdrawing the white rose broach. She pinned it onto the dress just at the throat.

Life was becoming full of possibilities, and she wasn't going to turn back now that she was moving forward.

STANDING BEFORE THE mirror, Auggie adjusted the royal blue tie then brushed away any lint that may have settled on his steel gray vest and matching trousers. He slid out his pocket watch checking the time: five-thirty, time to get underway. Placing the watch back into the vest pocket, he made sure the chain lay perfectly.

He'd bitten the bullet earlier in the day and gone to the barber to have his hair and beard professionally trimmed. For a fleeting moment while sitting in the chair, he had considered having his entire beard shaven off then reconsidered, deciding he wasn't ready to reveal that part of himself just yet. Not until he knew if there was any hope for him with Elizabeth.

It was then he realized he would like to

officially begin courting her. He was unsure as to how it was done here in the West. If he were back East, he'd present himself to her family and state his intentions. The young lady's family would then require a chaperone accompany them on every outing but only if the lady being courted was under twenty-one. Lucky for him, Elizabeth didn't require a chaperone any longer.

Outside of courting Elizabeth, he wasn't clear in his mind, or his heart, exactly what he wanted beyond that. It was obvious to him that she still mourned for her late husband. To anyone paying attention, it would be clear by the sadness in her eyes on the rare occasion she spoke of him. Her late husband was a subject he tried not to broach unless she brought it up first.

All that didn't matter. He wanted to get to know her more. He hoped she would feel the same way about him.

Slipping on his suit jacket, Auggie left his apartment then jogged down the stairs. A shrill whistle met him when he reached the lobby.

"You look quite handsome, Mr. Raines." Mary winked, a bouquet of colorful wildflowers in her hand.

"Do you have a secret admirer I don't know about, Mrs. Hall?" Auggie teased back, knowing full well Mary had long ago decided to stay a widow for the rest of her days.

"By all means no!" Mary laughed, handing him the bouquet. "You can't very well pick a young lady up without flowers. Or have you forgotten how it's done?"

Auggie blushed, for he had indeed forgotten. "You are always on top of these matters," he complimented, relieving her of the blooms. "Thank you, Mary."

"Now remember your manners. And don't—"

"Don't press her about plans for the future," Auggie finished for her. It had been exactly what he'd been reminding himself of for days. In fact, every minute for the last few hours if he were honest with himself.

"Well, I think you just might have this under control after all." Mary winked. "Have a nice dinner and don't keep her out too late," she said on her way back to the kitchen.

Auggie smiled then set out to pick up his dinner companion.

Dinner companion—it had been many years since he'd had a beautiful woman on his arm for the evening. He was rather looking forward to it.

With any luck, tonight would be the first of many to come. As long as their working relationship wasn't strained by it. He'd really rather not have to look for another seamstress now that the service was doing so well.

Mostly he didn't want to attempt to get through a day without seeing Elizabeth. He'd gotten rather used to seeing her every day now that she was part of the Grand family.

Auggie turned the corner of the path leading to Elizabeth's row house. Passing the church, he paused for a moment. Closing his eyes, he said a silent prayer giving thanks for all God had provided them with and for an enjoyable evening yet to come. He also included that if anyone deserved to be treated to a night out on the town it was Elizabeth Hamilton.

Auggie continued the short distance to Elizabeth's porch. Drawing in a breath to calm his quaking nerves, he knocked on the door then took a step back. After several moments, it swung open and his heart sank.

"Willa, is Elizabeth well?" he asked, hoping she wasn't for why else would Willa be here?

"Yes, she is quite well," Willa answered, stepping around him. "Elizabeth will be right here."

"Thank you," he said, watching Willa take the path back to town.

When he turned back to the door, he sucked in his breath. Before him was the most beautiful angel he'd ever seen. His heart pounded. Blood raced like fire through his veins. His hands were sweating so badly he almost dropped the bouquet.

The blue stripes of the form-fitting shirtwaist matched her eyes. And the way her hair set softly upon her head looked like a halo. She was his angel; he felt it in his heart.

"You are a beautiful vision," he finally said, his hands shaking as he held out the flowers.

Elizabeth smiled, her eyes sparkling and her cheeks blushing a lovely pale pink. "Thank you. Please come in while I put them in water. It'll only take a moment."

"Are you sure?" he asked, nervous about what people might say.

"Yes, I'm quite sure." Elizabeth walked into the house leaving him to contemplate as to whether or not to follow. "Are you coming in?"

Auggie swallowed hard then entered but left the door open. The room felt homey and comfortable. Just as Elizabeth was, everything was neat as a pin.

"If I may be so bold to say, the color of your dress looks good on you. That is to say it goes well with your complexion." Auggie suddenly felt awkward. Had he said it wrong? He really wanted to tell her how he admired the way the style fit her curves like a glove.

"Thank you," she said, placing the vase of flowers on the table. "It is one of my earlier creations. I'm afraid it may be out of fashion."

"Nonsense! The craftsmanship is exquisite," he said, stepping aside for her to pass over the threshold.

"I am a bit out of practice," she laughed, waiting on the porch as he closed the door.

An idea came to Auggie as he automatically offered her his arm. He was pleasantly surprised when she slipped her hand around through his elbow as they strolled down the path to Blessings Valley.

ELIZABETH WASN'T SURE what the difference between now and weeks earlier was or when the change had happened, but she felt quite comfortable being escorted by Auggie into town. She'd even received a nod of approval from Fannie as she closed the church doors.

"It's a lovely night," Elizabeth commented, not knowing what else to say. It was different at the

Grand where they had the hotel and her work to discuss. This outing was something entirely different. It was a private, personal experience.

Her heart skipped a beat when Auggie gazed down at her, smiling. "Yes, it is. I hope you won't be too chilled on the way home; it may turn cooler once the night has settled in."

"I have my shawl. It's not that long of a walk back." She returned his smile, warmed by his concern. "Of course, I could always stay at Willa's if I needed to. But I don't think that will be necessary, do you?"

"I promise to get you home at a reasonable hour." Auggie chuckled, placing his hand over hers.

They walked the remaining distance to Millie's Café, nodding at those they met along the way. Elizabeth knew they would most likely be the talk of the Blessings Valley by morning yet she didn't care—much. It felt good to do something remotely normal even if some may think it was far too soon for such activities.

She finally accepted she had every right to have dinner with a man as nice as Auggie Raines. The fact that he was a friend made him an easy person to spend a bit of social time with. There were no expectations of progressing to a love match. True love only came once in a lifetime, not twice.

Elizabeth felt everyone's speculating gazes on them as they entered Millie's. Auggie guided her over to a table where they could have a somewhat private conversation yet not so secluded as to invoke any more gossip than necessary. At least no one could consider he was after a rich widow's money, as it was far from the truth. Would they think she was after the successful hotel owner's bank roll?

It wasn't like he was rich. Auggie was a businessman doing just as well as the other businesses in Blessings Valley. He may be able to live comfortably, but he was a far cry from being rich. At least, that was Elizabeth's opinion, having worked with him for the past several months.

"Good evening, what can I get you?" a familiar voice asked, causing Elizabeth to look up in surprise.

"Viv!" Elizabeth exclaimed, jumping up to embrace her friend. Vivian Hickcock had lost her husband Matt in the same mining accident Elizabeth had lost Steven. "When did you start working here?"

Vivian hugged her back, smiling. "Not long ago. I needed the money so here I am."

"I understand. Always remember you are stronger than you think," Elizabeth encouraged sitting back down.

"Thank you." Vivian continued to smile, her pencil poised to take an order. "Are you ready to order?"

"I think the broiled ham and scalloped potatoes, if Elizabeth is agreeable," Auggie suggested his eyes on Elizabeth in question.

Elizabeth's heart melted a bit more. He was taking her opinion into consideration. In truth, her stomach had pinched with hunger when she had looked at the menu. He had chosen the meal responsible for that reaction of hunger.

"I believe that is an excellent choice," Elizabeth agreed, smiling first at Auggie then at Viv.

"Would it be possible to get a pot of coffee as well?" Auggie asked.

"I'll ask Cook, but I can't guarantee you'll have a pot of your own," Vivian offered, writing the request on the order form.

"Fair enough," Auggie stated.

"Thank you, Viv." Elizabeth smiled as her friend turned to deliver their order to the kitchen. She was glad to see a few of her fellow widows were starting to carve out a life for themselves. She knew firsthand the struggle Vivian had to be going through in order to stay in her home.

Turning her attention back to Auggie, sadness knocked at the wall of defense she'd erected the past few months. "Even though I rarely see her, Viv lives near me. Her husband Matt was killed in the mining accident as well. I certainly didn't expect to see anyone I know here. I mean, I haven't eaten anywhere but home since the funeral. And avoided as many people as possible when I came into town."

"I remember seeing his name in the obituaries." Auggie said quietly. "Blessings Valley is a small town, Elizabeth. If you look around the room, you most likely know everyone here."

Elizabeth scanned the room. Shaking her head, she had to disagree. "Not everyone. Even though I know who some people are, there are only a few that I feel I really 'know'.

"Take you for instance. I really didn't know who you were before I started working at the Grand,

and why would I have? There was no reason to. I was a happily married—I was busy being a wife to a wonderful man." She swallowed back the rock of sorrow lodged in her throat. "What I do know about you only goes as far as the Grand and Blessings Valley. If not for your kindness and faith in me, I may have had to return home. You've been a gracious employer not only with me but with all of the Grand employees. Everything before then is a mystery that you keep close to you."

"I could say the same of you," Auggie replied. "That door swings both ways, Elizabeth."

"Yes, it does, except it seems to stop at some point before swinging completely open." Elizabeth smiled. She knew he was right. They had their secrets—everyone did. What were his?

"One day it will open completely, but tonight is for you and all that you mean to the Grand." Auggie sat back in the chair, his gaze pinning her in hers.

The Grand? What I mean to the hotel? The disappointment edging its way into her heart surprised her. Why should she care if she was only important to the hotel and not to him?

"Like all of the employees?" Elizabeth shifted in her seat shaking away the hurt that had pierced her heart. "I am grateful that I am an asset to the Grand. My work as a seamstress has been a benefit, I'm sure. One that has served both of us well over the past several months."

"Elizabeth, that's not what—" Auggie began stumbling for his meaning.

"Your dinner will be here soon. In the meantime, here is the pot of coffee you requested."

Vivian placed the pot and two cups on the table, leaving Elizabeth wondering what Auggie really meant.

CHAPTER 13

Silence settled comfortably over them once their dinner had been served. Auggie watched as Elizabeth forked the last of her ham then followed her lead.

"Would you like more coffee?" he asked, having noticed her cup was nearly empty.

"Yes, thank you." She sat back in her chair looking like a cat who'd just finished a bowl of milk. He half expected to hear her purring at any moment.

"I hope you found the meal satisfying; it's one of Millie's specialties," he commented, pouring her a bit more of the dark brew. He purposely failed to mention it was also his favorite.

"It has been quite some time since I had something that reminded me of home. The brown sugar glaze was a nice surprise. My mother made it that way as well," Elizabeth said, her blue eyes gazing sadly at him over the rim of the porcelain cup.

"Where is home for you exactly? I remember you saying you were from Virginia, but that is all I know." He caught the sag of her shoulders. She must miss home during her time of mourning, especially a mother to lean on.

"Is it important?" Elizabeth cast her gaze down as if she were uncertain to reveal her past. "I suppose it must be since you are asking. I grew up on a working farm in Richmond, Virginia. I had to learn how to make my own clothes at an early age."

"That's quite resourceful, but didn't your family make enough to buy your clothes?" Auggie asked, then quickly wished he could take it back. Was she from a poor family? "Did you design them yourself or—"

"Auggie, I'm not sure you really want to hear all the details of my childhood." Elizabeth caressed the porcelain cup in a way Auggie thought must help keep her feelings in check. It was probably a distraction from facing unpleasant memories; he'd used the technique himself on more than one occasion.

"On the contrary, these are the type of things I would like to know if I am to expand your duties," Auggie said, surprised by his words. He really hadn't fully given any thought to expanding the seamstress services the hotel currently offered. Why was it the unexpected always seemed to happen when he was around Elizabeth?

"I would take a piece of unwanted clothing and transform it into something a little more fashionable," Elizabeth explained, averting her gaze from his. "It was a way to breathe new life into a hand-me-down at hardly any cost other than needle and thread. And maybe some buttons if I didn't have any in my button box that would work."

"How did you get the position at the dress shop?" Auggie immediately wondered if she'd told him the day of her interview. If she had then he'd forgotten.

"I was recommended by someone I had redesigned a dress for." Elizabeth looked up at him with pride in her eyes.

"Do you miss recreating a discarded piece of clothing?" Auggie asked. "I think it would give you some satisfaction to do so."

"I was able to work with my own clothing while I was married, so I kept the skill up some. Many times, I had to remake a skirt or a blouse that had become worn somewhere," Elizabeth said, a faraway look on her face. "It didn't bother me to have to do it. I was happy and loved my late husband very much. He worked hard in the mine, and it was my way of helping us save as much money as we could.

"Why is this important to you now after all these months that I've been working for you? Have I done something wrong?"

"No! I apologize if I've given you that impression," Auggie gushed. "It occurred to me that I hardly know anything about you. I wanted to explore the depth of your skills outside of mending torn garments."

"Is that why you asked me to dinner? If it was, you very well could have asked me at the hotel during work hours." Elizabeth's confused expression echoed in her words.

Auggie's hands suddenly felt clammy. For the first time in years, he was feeling awkward. He couldn't tell her why he was asking her when he didn't know himself the importance.

"Partly," he finally said, taking a deep breath to collect himself for a moment. He looked into her eyes full of questions and suddenly his words were gone. All he could do was stare at her hoping he could speak at some point. He was sure he looked a fool unable to answer her question.

"Are you ready for dessert?" Vivian asked, saving the awkward moment for him.

"Not for me, thank you, Viv," Elizabeth replied, placing her folded napkin next to her empty plate.

"I will pass as well," Auggie answered, feeling that he may have finally gotten ahold of his senses.

"I'll be right back with your check then." Vivian gathered up their plates, taking them to the kitchen.

"This has been nice, Auggie," Elizabeth said, her eyes bright with gratitude.

"It has at that," Auggie agreed happily. "It has been some time since I've taken a lady to dinner."

Vivian slipped him the check then turned to another table of diners.

"I promised to get you home early. Shall we?" Auggie rose then pulled out her chair for her.

Together, they paid the check and walked out of Millie's into the night, so many unanswered questions left at the table.

ELIZABETH COULDN'T SHAKE the feeling there was more to Auggie's questioning than he admitted to. Was her work not up to standards—his standards—anymore? Had he used tonight's dinner as a way to soften the blow of dismissing her? He'd been far too quick in saying she'd done nothing wrong. Well, she wasn't about to wait. She wanted to know now if she was to be sacked.

"Auggie, if I've done something to displease you, I wish you would say so," Elizabeth said point-blank. She hated beating around the bush about anything, it was so much better to be straightforward and honest.

"My dear Elizabeth, I already told you everything is fine," Auggie reassured her squeezing her hand. "I promise you, there is no need for you to be concerned."

"I know what you said, but I still can't help but think—" Elizabeth began, swallowing down words that would hurt her. She loved working at the Grand. The people she saw each day, had conversations with, ate meals with had become her family and she desperately needed a family now.

"The truth of it is that I'd like for us to be friends besides just at the hotel," Auggie said, stopping to look down at her. There was sincerity in his eyes—and hope. The kind of hope that she didn't know if she'd ever be able to give him, or any man for that matter.

"What are you saying exactly?" Elizabeth asked, afraid of what the answer would be. He had to know she wasn't looking for a husband. Or anything other than a platonic friendship.

"We get on quite well, don't we?" he asked.

"Yes, I believe we do," Elizabeth agreed, feeling a knot form in her stomach. "I have discovered I enjoy coming to the hotel every day and seeing everyone."

"Including me?" Auggie teased.

"Including you." Elizabeth laughed. "Sometimes you can be so amusing, Auggie. I like that about you."

"Well, that is a start," Auggie said. "Does that mean you are agreeable to let the world know we are truly friends both at work and away?"

"Friends, yes. Anything more than that, no," Elizabeth said honestly, suddenly noticing they were in front of the church. A few more steps and she'd be home. "Goodness, are we nearly there already?"

"How did that happen?" Auggie chuckled. "The night is ending far too quickly for me. I had a wonderful evening with you, Elizabeth."

"So did I, Auggie, it was a lovely evening." Elizabeth shook his hand then walked up her porch steps. "Thank you again."

"Maybe we can to it again soon?" Auggie said, hope reflecting on his moonlit face.

"Maybe." She smiled, opening her door. "Good night, Auggie."

"Good night, Elizabeth."

Elizabeth closed and locked the door then lit a lantern. The flowers on the table looked as fresh as they had when Auggie had given them to her just a few hours ago. Even in the shadows of the lantern, the blooms brought color into the darkness. Color signified life. Life she realized she wanted to rediscover.

"He really is a nice man," she said aloud more to herself than anyone else. Well, maybe she was telling Steven as well. The thought of him being able to hear her was still a comfort to her heart. She supposed one day she'll come to discover that she talked to him less and less each day except when something important happened. Then even that may fade away too.

Lantern lighting the way, she went up the stairs to her bedroom. She'd have tomorrow to do as she pleased for the first time in well over a month. She could sleep in if she desired—as if she would anyway. Maybe she'd find a dress from the back of her wardrobe to redesign. If she did and completed it to her satisfaction, she'd wear it to the hotel

Slipping out of her dress and into an old, comfy night gown, Elizabeth splashed water on her face. She gazed into the mirror, pulling the pins from her hair. Shaking her hair loose, she gasped at the reflection smiling back at her.

Steven!

Whirling around, she discovered she was alone. Frantically turning back to the mirror, she was astonished to find that this time the reflection smiling back at her was her own.

For the first time since the accident, since she'd gotten the news that her beloved Steven was dead, since he'd been laid to rest, she looked as happy as she was beginning to feel.

And all because of Auggie Raines.

WHERE IN THE world had the thought of adding to Elizabeth's duties come from? If anything, he'd much rather lessen her duties so he could find a way to spend more time with her.

When he'd seen the brief sparkle in her eyes as she spoke of how she would transform used throwaway clothes into something wearable must have gotten him thinking. It made sense in a mining town like Blessings Valley to be able to offer the service of making over clothes to the single miners for a reasonable and affordable fee.

The men who slaved away in the mines were proud and worked hard for everything they had by going deep into the ground for the likes of him. They shunned handouts of charity no matter how well intended they were or how low their own lives were.

After seeing how Elizabeth lived—a nice but small home that was sparse and simply furnished— he was beginning to understand their plight. He began to understand their struggle to put food on the table. Their joy of being together at the end of each day's end.

If he could be so fortunate.

If all the mining families were as proud and self-sufficient as Elizabeth, then Blessings Valley was blessed to have them living here among them.

The question—the first of many important ones—was how he could be of service to Elizabeth and the town's folk.

The meager sewing room wouldn't be sufficient once it was fully equipped with everything that was needed. And that was the other dilemma; what does a dress shop need? Is it the same as a tailor? He'd only seen the inside of his tailor's as far as a room to be measured in. What lay behind that was a mystery.

Then there was the question of how to convince Elizabeth to accept his offer. In truth, what was he offering her other than to remain an employee with increased responsibilities? What kind of an offer was that? One that she would turn down flat and he didn't blame her if she did.

He wasn't sure if it was one he'd take himself, that's for sure.

If he could come up with a plan, would Elizabeth agree to a partnership? She'd definitely expressed interest in one day having her own shop and had inquired about how to get a loan.

Would she be open if he offered her an investment loan? If she really desired her own dress shop, he couldn't imagine she'd refuse his offer.

Picking up the pace, Auggie reached the steps of the Grand and took them two at a time. His heart raced with excitement as he strolled through the lobby then into his office. Sitting at his desk he found a blank piece of paper and began drawing the layout of the Grand.

Turning the page clockwise several times it suddenly struck him. There was enough room at the front of the hotel to build a dress shop. Why hadn't he seen it before?

"Raines, you are a genius!" Smiling he placed the drawing in the middle desk drawer for safe keeping.

Turning out the light, he closed the door then

headed for his apartment. He climbed the stairs whistling a gay tune feeling like bricks were lifted off his shoulders.

He just may have found a way to keep Elizabeth near him for a very long time.

CHAPTER 14

Elizabeth decided to go visit Willa. It was her day off, and she'd already done the chores this morning. Maybe Willa could help her make sense of Auggie's comments last night, because she certainly couldn't; and she'd tried to do so all night.

After a restless night's sleep, she'd gone over the past few days and couldn't come up with a reason why Auggie would want to dismiss her. Every garment had been repaired with perfection.

Why the sudden interest in her past? He certainly didn't need to take her to dinner only to ask about her dressmaking abilities.

Willa would know—she always seemed to.

Setting out on the well-travelled path into the heart of Blessings Valley, Elizabeth paused for a moment in front of the church. After several moments, she turned to go when her name drifted out to her.

Looking back, Fannie stood in the door, a small

smile on her face.

"Good morning, Fannie" Elizabeth called out returning to the bottom of the church steps, still not willing to go inside again. She had once but only because she feared Fannie was hurt or needed help. At least that's what she kept telling herself each time she paused at God's House.

"Hello Elizabeth!" Fannie answered walking to the top of the steps. "He's a God-fearing man, Elizabeth. One that you need in your life."

Elizabeth starred at her, puzzled by Fannie's odd remark. "Who are you referring to?"

"Why Mr. Raines of course." Fannie answered her gaze sending a shiver down Elizabeth's spine. "Everyone knows he is sweet on you."

"No, you are wrong. Mr. Raines is my employer." Elizabeth insisted shaking her head. "He is not sweet on me, Fannie."

"Open your heart and you shall see the truth." Fannie answered then returned to the hallows of the church.

"Dear Merciful Lord, please look after Fannie." Elizabeth prayed quietly continuing on her trek. She envied Fannie for having something she had so much faith in. She did once. Would she again?

Could she open her heart fully to her faith and to love? She didn't know if it were possible anymore.

Reaching Willa's boardinghouse, Elizabeth was surprised to see her sitting on the porch swing. Was she waiting for her?

"I was wondering how long before you arrived." Willa greeted Elizabeth at the top step.

"You wish to talk about something? Or someone?"

"I don't know how you always know when I'm troubled, but you do." Elizabeth remarked neither confirming nor denying her question.

"My dear, all one has to do is look into your face." Willa stepped aside, "Now come in for a bit of breakfast."

Elizabeth nodded then followed her friend and confidant through the rooms of the boardinghouse. All was so quiet that she heard the tick tock of the grandfather clock in the front parlor. Was it a sign her life was ticking away like the second hand of the clock? No, she was only letting her imagination get the best of her.

"Come Elizabeth and tell me what is on your mind." Willa stated as they walked into her kitchen. "Did you not have a nice dinner with Auggie?"

Elizabeth sat in hopes of calming the fear bubbling in her tummy. Had she become the subject of town gossip? From what Fannie said, Elizabeth believed so. Of course, that is if it were true.

"That's the problem. Dinner was very—nice. And he is very easy to be with. I rather enjoyed myself and Auggie's company. That is until Auggie's questioning took me by surprise." Elizabeth accepted the cup of coffee and pastry offered. "Thank you."

"I would venture to guess he is curious about you." Willa smiled sitting across from her. "Do you remember what it was like when Steven first started to court you? The many questions he asked about your family, your desires, your plans for the future."

"It's not the same," Elizabeth whispered,

blinking away tears. "Auggie's questioning was about my skills for dressmaking. Why now after all these months would he suddenly care about my skills. Unless he does only want to increase my duties, as he said. Thankfully he is *not* interested in me as a love interest. Maybe a friend, but not a love interest."

"I don't believe that, Elizabeth. What I do believe is that he is interested in you as more than an employee." Willa stirred her coffee then took a sip, slowly. "I know you must know that when a man asks questions that he is thinking about whether or not to court the woman in question."

"Fannie said he is sweet on me. I thought I had made it clear to him that I wasn't interested in having a relationship with another man." Elizabeth insisted, playing with the pastry crumbs on her saucer. "I lost my husband. The only man I ever gave my heart to. There isn't anything left for another."

"That is something that you will one day have to re-evaluate, Elizabeth." Willa smiled picking up their soiled plates and placing them in the huge sink.

"How so?" Elizabeth asked her voice filled with determination. "My life has no room for another. I'll *never* marry again; can't you understand that? I don't have any idea why I should reconsider anything."

"Because you may be throwing away a second chance at happiness and love." Willa said point blank.

"I don't believe in love coming around twice.

And I'm not so desperate as to take a man as a husband so he can provide for me. I'm capable of doing that myself now. I've proven that." Elizabeth whispered, tears flowing down her cheeks. "True love comes only once, Willa."

AUGGIE SAT IN his office contemplating how he was going to explain any construction work on the hotel. He could say he decided to add a men's smoking lounge, but that could leave the ladies feeling left out. Although there was enough land in the back he owned where a garden could go.

He would of course keep everything closed off as much as possible from prying eyes and curious minds. He'd send for construction workers and provide them accommodations and meals as partial payment for their work.

As for the garden, he could hire local so that any suspicion—and there was likely to be some— would be kept at a minimum. Satisfied with the decisions he'd made this morning he leaned back in the chair and closed his eyes. Before long he drifted away.

They were racing across his father's land. Each of them having had maybe one to many drafts that afternoon. Then the bet that Auggie's new mount wasn't as fast as he claimed him to be. A wager was made and accepted.

His horse stumbled. Auggie flew out of the saddle landing against one of the great oak trees. Blood ran down the side of his face and neck. Pain seared through his head. Shouts of concern. Then darkness came.

A blinding light. Voices. He'd been lucky. Scarred for life. He was alive. It could have been a lot worse.

Then kind blue eyes smiled at him.

Auggie woke with a start, his brow moist with sweat. His breathing labored. Panic soared through him. It had been some time since he'd relived that awful day.

"A dream, just a dream," he gasped for air until he finally breathed normal. Touching his face he found the scar hidden under the beard.

He was still safe. Safe from ridicule. Safe from rejection.

"Coffee. I need coffee." He said pushing away from the desk. He knew Mary was in the kitchen as he'd heard the clanking of pots echoing not long ago. The aroma of coffee drifting in reached his senses. Breathing deeply he absorbed the rich scent. He definitely needed the coffee.

It was going to be a quiet day without Elizabeth here to talk with. This was the first time he'd missed, really missed her. He began to realize how much he looked forward to seeing her each day she came to the hotel. And their dinner last night—

Is that what sparked the dream? His insecurities about how he was beginning to feel. Yet it was those blue eyes in the end that woke him from the recurring nightmare.

Had Elizabeth's blue eyes saved him?

"You look like death warmed over!" Mary exclaimed as he walked into the kitchen. "Did you get any sleep at all?"

"Some," Auggie smiled, snatching a muffin

from a plate.

"I hope you got Elizabeth home at a respectable hour." Mary scolded handing him a cup of coffee.

"Have no fear. She arrived at her doorstep safe and sound." Auggie said adding some cream to the brew.

"And last night?" Mary fished.

"What about it?" Auggie tensed, sensing she wanted to know every detail of their dinner.

"For pity sake. Did you have a nice time?" Mary stood hands on her hips waiting for an answer.

"Yes, I had a very nice time. Dinner was pleasant." Auggie answered hedging around her question.

"Pleasant? Is that the best you can do? What did you talk about?" Mary continued not giving up.

"Is it important?" Auggie asked drinking the coffee. It wasn't like Mary to ask so many questions, until recently that is. He wondered what she was up to.

"Yes, to a woman that conversation is very important. It tells her what a man's intentions are or could be." Mary enlightened, sitting across the table from him. "Conversation can be the first step to courtship between two unmarried people. Of course, you've had plenty of opportunity to strike up a conversation these past few months."

"I asked her about her skills as a dressmaker. That I was thinking of expanding her duties." Auggie said feeling rather proud of himself for asking something personal but not too personal.

"You did not!" Mary gasped, her hand on her

heart in shock. "How could you say such a thing Augustine?"

Auggie sat stumped. What in blazes had he done wrong? He'd been straightforward and honest. Well mostly.

"Say what exactly?"

"Tell her you are considering adding more work onto her already busy day?" Mary spat, pushing away from the table and standing over him. "Do you have any idea what you said?"

"No, not really." Auggie replied trying to sort things out. "Why are you so angry? It was a safe and informative conversation."

"Informative for who? You told her that you value her work and as a reward you are giving her more to do. And you did it over dinner of all places." Mary huffed stomping her foot. "You have probably lost your only chance—"

"Chance at what?" Auggie questioned hoping she wouldn't say the one thing he had been avoiding by coming out West. Love.

"Ooooo, never mind!" Mary walked back over to the oven banging around several pots. "Go back to your office Augustine. I can't talk to you right now."

Auggie took his cup of coffee and went back to his office in total confusion. What had he said that was so wrong? He'd thought he handled dinner with Elizabeth perfectly.

Could she have misunderstood his intention regarding her duties at the Grand? He hadn't mentioned—oh now he began to understand what Mary had meant.

Explaining his idea of adding to her duties must have sounded like that's why he'd taken her out to dinner last night. To soften the blow of being assigned more work.

Looking down at his sketch he knew what he said was quite different from what he had meant. But he couldn't tell her that.

Not yet anyway.

"MR. RAINES," ELIZABETH marched into Auggie's office doing her best to remain composed. "I believe we need to discuss your future plans for me here at the Grand."

"Elizabeth! I didn't expect you today, but what a wonderful surprise. What are you doing here?" Auggie stammered shoving some papers together. "I thought we were well past being formal with each other."

The smile on his face both irritated and excited her. Distracted for a moment, she'd forgotten her reason for the visit.

"We had, until last night." Elizabeth answered keeping her resolve firm. She mustn't show any real emotion, not now. She had to remind him she was a strong, no nonsense woman.

"Please sit down. Tell me how last night has changed things between us." Auggie motioned at the empty chair. "Would you like some coffee? I'll have Stewart get some for you."

"No thank you." Elizabeth sat staring at him across the desk. "I thought we were becoming friends. But after what you said last night, I think I was wrong."

"No, you aren't wrong. We are friends as far as I'm concerned." Auggie said a certain apprehension in his eyes. "How do you think it has changed?"

Elizabeth thought it would be easy to confront him. Now she was finding it to be anything but. A sadness she'd not felt before swept over her. One she couldn't explain even to herself. She didn't want to leave the Grand. More to the point, she looked forward to coming every day and seeing Stewart, Mary, and the others. Auggie in particular.

"When you took me to dinner just to tell me you are thinking of giving me more work." Elizabeth reminded him. Surely, he hadn't forgotten in less than twenty-four hours what he'd told her. "It was something you could have done here and saved both money and time."

"Yes, about that." Auggie looked away avoiding making eye contact with her.

"Yes, about that." Elizabeth repeated a bit sarcastic wondering what lie he was manufacturing. "It is my future you are talking about."

Auggie cleared his throat nervously playing with his pencil. He's hiding something, but what?

"First let me assure you that your future with the Grand is yours for as long as you like." Auggie replied annoyingly taping the pencil on the edge of his desk. "I am thinking of a few changes. I wanted your assistance, nothing more."

"What kind of changes are you considering making?" Elizabeth asked not sure if he was only covering for last night. Or if he really meant that he wanted her help.

"Would you consider having a late breakfast

with me to discuss it?" That twinkle was back in his eye. He was up to something; she could feel it.

He'd left her with two choices. She could refuse and be left in the dark. Or she could accept his invitation and find out what was going on. She had been leaving the dark behind and had no intention of going back—ever.

"Yes, I'll have breakfast with you." Elizabeth agreed praying she was doing the right thing. If this was a trap, he was laying it out with perfection and she was stepping into it eyes wide open.

"Great! Give me a few minutes to inform Stewart I'll be out for a while." Auggie smiled, rising out of the chair, then paused looking down at her. Warmth spread over her in places reserved for the man she'd loved. "On second thought, let's go together."

"Alright." Elizabeth stood as he opened the door. As she passed him, he offered up his arm. For a moment she thought of rejecting it, instead she smiled wrapping her hand around it.

"Stewart," Auggie said as they stopped at the lobby desk. "Elizabeth and I will be out for a few hours. If you need me, we will be at Millie's. I'll let you know when we've returned."

"Yes, sir." Stewart nodded a large smile on his face.

"Do you realize you just referred to me as Elizabeth and not Mrs. Hamilton to Stewart?" Elizabeth said surprised by the slip of the tongue. That's all it had to be…a slip.

"I do. It's about time we let the world know we are friends." Auggie smiled patting her hand. "Do you agree?"

"We'll see after you tell me what's on your mind whether or not we are still friends." Elizabeth said a warm cozy feeling covering her heart.

CHAPTER 15

Auggie watched Elizabeth's every expression. Smiling he took a spoonful of the rolled oats with apples and cream.

"This is delicious," Elizabeth smiled. "I've not had anything that tasted so perfect."

"I have to say that I agree with you," Auggie finished his last spoonful then pushed the bowl aside. "If not for Mary's cooking, I'd be here every meal."

"I can see why. Both Mary and Millie have skills that rival each other." Elizabeth dabbed her mouth with the napkin then sat back eyeing him.

Auggie felt her gaze judge him completely. She waited for him to explain, rather dig himself out of the hole he'd dug last night.

"I apologize if I misled you at dinner. It was not my intention to do so." Auggie placed his napkin on the table counting his blessings she was willing to allow him to at least come up with an explanation, of sorts.

"That's why we are here, for you to tell me what you really meant." Elizabeth raised an eyebrow at him.

"I would like you to assist in planning a garden. That's what I meant by more duties." Auggie began climbing out of that hole. "It will take a woman's touch. I hope that the ladies of Blessings Valley will hold garden parties there."

"And it would give guests a place to relax or have a quiet conversation." Elizabeth added, her face softening into the smile he'd grown to love.

Love? Yes love! He found that warm, inviting smile of hers was something he loved about her.

"Among other reasons to enjoy it, yes." Auggie agreed thinking of the many stolen kisses that may take place among the blooms.

Elizabeth blushed a lovely shade of pink. He'd have to send for some roses that matched the shade so every time he saw them, he'd think of her.

"What do you have in mind?" Elizabeth asked, her eyes filled with curiosity.

"A shelter or gazebo out of the sun where guests could have tea or read or just sit in peace." Auggie suggested off the top of head after remembering what his mother's garden had looked like. "A small walking path if there is room. I don't have a large enough piece of property in the back for anything overly extravagant."

"You'll need some shrubs to offer some privacy for anyone who takes a stroll." Elizabeth offered. "And flowers that are not only pleasant to smell but also to look at. That will survive the heat of the summers here when there can be a lack of rain for weeks."

"With enough green space to play lawn games." Auggie said as an afterthought.

"I thought this was for the ladies?" Elizabeth scrutinized, then laughed. "Do you think they'll only want to play croquette?"

"Well, I would hope they would. If they want more than tapping a ball around the grounds or anything else a garden can offer then they need to either go home or register in the hotel." Auggie grinned, knowing full well what Elizabeth was getting at. Some may want to use the privacy for a little intimacy with their walking partners.

"How much land do you have to work with?" Elizabeth inquired a small grin on her soft pink lips.

"I believe a third of an acre." Auggie calculated in his head. "That should give us plenty of room to accommodate our purposes. If not and more is needed, then I'll purchase what we need."

"I think we should starting planning then, don't you?" Elizabeth had that sparkle back in her eyes. The one that always made him feel everything was going to be fine and right. But could he trust the feeling with his heart?

"So I have redeemed myself in your eyes?" Auggie smiled, hoping he must have but wanted to hear it from her.

"Yes, Auggie, you have." Elizabeth smiled, finishing the last of her tea.

Auggie waved for the waitress and paid for their meal.

"When do you plan to get started?" Auggie

asked, anxious to spend more time with her. If they worked closely on the details then he may be able to learn things about her he otherwise wouldn't be able to.

"How about this afternoon?" Elizabeth suggested.

"You won't mind spending your day off working?" Auggie held back the joy reaching his heart.

"For this? Not at all." Elizabeth stated getting up from the table and leaving him to pay the check.

"A GARDEN!" ELIZABETH whispered standing outside of Millie's waiting for Auggie. Visions of scrolled metal benches, a table for two under a gazebo surrounded by flowering trees, an arbor draped with a lush vine. Couples strolling along a path discussing whatever young couples in love discuss. It could be a place for weddings as well during the spring and fall.

"Are you ready to get to work, Elizabeth?" Auggie asked offering his arm.

"Yes," Elizabeth accepted his arm and they started to head back over to the hotel. Glancing across the street, Smith's Dry Goods grabbed her attention and beckoned.

"Do you mind if we go to Smith's first? I'd like to inspect their seed inventory." Elizabeth asked re-routing their journey. "Get an idea of what we might be able to have planted."

"Not at all," Auggie chuckled, once again taking the lead. "Smith's may even have a mail-order catalogue you can look at."

"That would be wonderful!" Elizabeth smiled. *He really is thoughtful. How could I think badly of him? Because I jump to conclusions. Because he isn't—Stop it, Elizabeth!*

Reaching Smith's, Elizabeth sprung up the steps with Auggie in tow. She couldn't wait to take a look at the catalogues and start to pick out garden furniture. Anything to get her mind off the past and focused on the future.

"Mr. Raines. Mrs. Hamilton. Good to see you both again." Mr. Smith greeted from behind the counter a small grin on his face.

"Mr. Smith," Elizabeth said ignoring the smile hoping it meant nothing other than a greeting. Why should it mean anything more than that? She was being silly. "Do you happen to have any flower seed packets?"

"And a mail-order catalogue?" Auggie added as Elizabeth started to scour the nearby shelves.

"I happen to have two that you can look at, which would you prefer?" Mr. Smith asked reaching under the counter and producing the two catalogues.

"Let's start with Montgomery Ward, if it is one of them," Elizabeth called out looking over at the two men standing around casually. "Where did you say the seeds were kept?"

"On the shelf behind you and to your left, Mrs. Hamilton." Mr. Raines instructed.

Elizabeth sorted through the seeds, disappointed at not finding what she thought would be nice for the Grand garden. When Auggie said he planned on putting one in she pictured an arbor of beautiful light purple flowers. Now she was certain they'd have to order the plants from one of the catalogues and hope they arrived in planting condition.

She'd really hoped she'd been able to get started growing something right away, instead she returned to the front counter empty handed and disappointed.

"Have you found anything interesting?" Elizabeth asked standing next to Auggie gazing over his arm. The page was turned to men's fashions and which nothing to do with gardens.

"I looked but I wouldn't know it if I had come across anything useful or not." Auggie laughed. "Which is why I need your input. Did you find anything worth planting?"

Elizabeth sighed. "No, I'm afraid what I have in mind may not be possible."

"All things are possible, Elizabeth." Auggie said putting an arm around her shoulder and drawing her in.

What is he doing? She thought seeing the surprised look on Mr. Smith's face. *Has he gone mad and forgotten we are in public? No, he's been familiar on purpose but why?*

"Did you see an arbor while you leafed through the pages?" Elizabeth asked, moving the catalogue in front of her and flipped through the pages. She managed to put some distance between them. It felt like something was missing now but she kept her attention on the pages passing through her vision.

"I believe I did, as well as a nice gazebo." Auggie asked taking her hint and moving a few inches from her. "Why don't we go back to the office and discuss the plans for it?"

"Are you thinking of adding a garden to the Grand, Mr. Raines?" Mr. Smith inquired, that damn smile back on his face. Elizabeth was sure he was already calculating the possible order.

"Elizabeth is helping me in designing one," Auggie remarked, his smile sending heat down her spine.

"Mr. Raines has asked me to help with the design. Nothing more," Elizabeth said, establishing as sense of formality once again.

"Thank you, Mr. Smith, for your assistance." Elizabeth smiled and walked out of the store. She had to get some air for moment.

To get her pounding heart under control.

"TODAY IS YOUR day off, Elizabeth." Auggie felt a bit guilty for having dominated some of her private time. However, she'd been the one to come into his office this morning, demanding an explanation. Well, not demanding quite but just the same strongly insisting. "Would you allow me to walk you back home? We can talk about the garden next time you are at the Grand. There's no real hurry after all."

"I thought you wanted to start on it right away," Elizabeth remarked, staring at him.

"If there's one thing I know it's that these things take time." Facing in the direction of her house, Auggie offered her his arm. "There are a number of things to be considered."

"Such as what?" Elizabeth wrapped her arm

through his, sending heat through his blood vessels. "We make the decision what to buy and order it. How can that be so hard?"

"Harder than people may think." Auggie chuckled. "First of all planning the layout; what you want to plant and where you want people to sit. Then there is finding the right work crew and giving them a timeframe to finish the garden. Finding the right plants for the soil so that I'm not replacing them each year. The last thing is purchasing the furniture."

"Oh, I thought you would get what you wanted and then put things into storage." Elizabeth scrunched her face in a way that made her look like an adorable young lady. The urge to kiss the tip of her turned up nose overwhelmed him.

"If there was a place to store the furniture maybe, but there isn't." Auggie said, trying to keep from insulting her intelligence. All the storage space in the hotel was full; there wasn't room for more. "It's not the right time to plant flowers. At least I don't think it is. That's why I need to consult with someone who knows these things."

"I see." Disappointment echoed in Elizabeth's voice. "I guess I got a bit too excited."

"We both may have," Auggie said, accepting some of the blame himself. He'd had to come up with the lie of the garden to keep from losing her.

They continued walking in comfortable silence, each in their own thoughts. When Auggie glanced up the sun gleamed off the church cross in the distance.

"Elizabeth, may I ask you something?" Auggie

hesitated a moment. He may be pushing things, but he wanted to know why she seemed to hurry pass the church. He'd noticed it the few times they'd walked together on the path. He wasn't an every Sunday church goer, but he worshipped when he could.

"You may ask. No guarantee I'll answer." Elizabeth looked like she really didn't want to answer any questions concerning herself. After dinner last night, he really didn't blame her.

"I have noticed that you always seem to hurry past the church each time I've walked with you." Auggie said. "I was wondering why."

"I'm not sure you would understand." Elizabeth looked up at him, a deep sadness in her eyes. "Because I haven't forgiven yet."

"Forgiven?" Auggie asked confused. What did the church have to do with her forgiveness? "Who and what needs your forgiveness?"

"Does it matter?" Elizabeth asked, slipping her arm out of his. "It's a private matter."

A wave of coolness touched him and he longed for her warm touch to return.

"I don't mean to pry. It was only an observation. I was a bit curious is all," Auggie explained feeling there was more but didn't want to push her. He wanted to redeem himself in her eyes. "Would you be interested in dining with me again tonight around five o'clock? I promise not to talk about work."

"Dinner?" Elizabeth asked, looking at him like he'd lost his mind. "We just had a late breakfast, and you're thinking of food again?"

"All this talk about the garden has given me an appetite, I guess." Auggie exaggerated wishing she'd take his arm again. He wasn't ready to let her go yet today. "Didn't it make you hungry?"

Elizabeth laughed and he felt the tension between them lessen.

"Not at the moment," she said, a smile back on her face.

"I want to make it up to you." Auggie said, lightly touching her elbow. "My behavior last night wasn't exactly stellar. All I had on my mind was the Grand and expanding the business." He lied not wanting her to know just how badly he wanted to know everything about her.

"It wasn't you Auggie" Elizabeth began looking ahead of her and not at him. "It was your questions and the end result. At least where it was left at the end of the night."

"So it wasn't my behavior I need to be concerned about?" Auggie asked thankful that she had given him a reprieve.

"No it wasn't." Elizabeth smiled turning a pretty shade of pale pink that brightened her eyes.

She lowered her lashes shyly. *Is she flirting with me?* Chances were not, but he'd hold on to that tiny piece of hope anyway.

"Then you'll have dinner with me?" Auggie asked hopeful.

"Yes, I'll have dinner with you." Elizabeth smiled looping her arm around his once again.

CHAPTER 16

Elizabeth peered out the window at the crunching sound of wagon wheels. Opening the door she was surprised to find Auggie disembarking from a carriage dressed in jeans and a plaid shirt.

"Auggie, what in the world?" Elizabeth exclaimed standing on the porch in a blue cotton dress.

"Hello Elizabeth," Auggie greeted a warm smile on his face. "I thought we might do something different from last night. Are you willing for something that may be seen as unconventional?"

Elizabeth looked down at her dress wondering if she were a bit overdressed for what he might have in mind. This was definitely going to be a casual evening.

"Depends on what you mean by different."

"Well, I was thinking a ride through the countryside would be nice." Auggie began coming up the steps towards her. Her heart thumped so loud she thought he'd hear it for sure.

"I think I'd like that," she said. "Let me get my hat and then I'll be right out."

Auggie nodded as she went back inside.

A ride in the country? This will look like so much more than just a business relationship, if someone should see us. And I said I'd go. What is wrong with me? My Steven has only been gone for such a short time and I'm stepping out with another man!? Elizabeth hesitated to put her hat on as she gazed at her reflection in the mirror. For the first time in a long while she didn't look weary or tired. She looked almost—happy.

Tying the ribbon under her chin, she headed out the door. "I'm ready," she said taking Auggie's arm and then his hand as he helped her up into the carriage. The guilt she'd once hung onto left in the shadows of grief.

"Do you know where we are going?" she smiled watching him walk around and then climb into his side of the carriage.

"I thought we would just drive along until we got hungry." Auggie said, snapping the reins. "Walk on" he called out to the bay.

"That sounds nice. No worries. No timeline." Elizabeth said looking at him as he handled the horse with expertise. The way he commanded the horse with a gentle hand. Just as he conducted everything in his life. Gentle and with compassion. He was darn near perfect in her eyes.

"That is exactly what I am hoping for. The further away from prying eyes the more relaxed we both may be." He glanced over at her with hope in his eyes.

"Well I think that is exactly what is needed for us to get to know each other more." Elizabeth agreed as the Oklahoma countryside slowly went by. "You handle a horse and carriage fairly well."

"Thank you, I grew up on a horse ranch. I learned at a young age that quiet and gentle hands are best." Auggie smiled but there was a sadness in his eyes.

"That had to be wonderful to have some stability in your life." Elizabeth said thinking back on how chaotic her own life had been growing up.

"It was actually." Auggie's expression softened as those memories she could only imagine flooded him. "I love horses. Was an expert rider until..."

Elizabeth watched his face become ashen and remorse. "Until you came here and became a hotelier?"

"Yes, something like that." Auggie reined in near a stream. "How is this?"

Elizabeth looked around absorbing the fresh clean smells of being in the country brought. "I think it's a perfect spot."

Auggie tied off the horse, jumped out of the carriage and helped Elizabeth out. When she put her hand in his that warmth of familiarity spread through her again. How could he have this effect on her? He was her boss, and friend, nothing more. Never will be. She wasn't ready. Or was she?

"Why don't you pick a spot while I get the basket and blanket," Auggie said releasing her hand.

Turning away Elizabeth walked toward the

bank of the stream where a tree shaded a place from the sun. There were yellow flowers scattered along the grasses and around the trunk of the tree. Birds were chirping. Butterflies played among the blooms collecting nectar.

It was peaceful and perfect.

AUGGIE LIFTED A wicker basket and plaid blanket from the back of the carriage. When he turned around Elizabeth stood under the shade of the tree watching everything around her. She turned and the smile on her face was stunning. If only he could put that smile on her face every day. Maybe one day.

"This is a perfect place Auggie." She said walking slowly toward him.

Willing his body to move, he replied, "I was hoping you would like it. I come here when I need to get away from town and think."

"So, this where you've disappeared to from time-to-time." Elizabeth smiled. "If I'd known of this place I may have done the same thing over the past several months. It's peaceful."

Auggie handed her the basket then spread the blanket under the tree.

"Whatever is in here smells delicious!" Elizabeth placed the basket on the blanket. "Did Mary do this for you?"

"Yes, she did." Auggie took her hand and helped her to sit upon the blanket. "I believe there are sandwiches of some kind, salad, cheese, and tea as well."

Elizabeth spread her skirt around her as she found a comfortable position. Auggie found a spot near the tree trunk and settled in.

"Tell me about yourself, Elizabeth. Where do your people come from?" Auggie asked removing the tea and two cups from the basket.

"Thank you," Elizabeth nodded taking a cup then looked toward the stream for moment before meeting his gaze. "As far as I know my family is originally from Virginia. Mother told me when I was a baby we moved around a lot. My father was always looking for something better. He finally found it near Richmond, at least enough where he and mother put down some roots. Once I was old enough to go to school, mother put her foot down. She told him she was not going to move again. And if he thought of uprooting their family, he'd do it alone.

"Father relented and became successful enough, more than some I would guess. There was always food on the table and money for used clothing." She looked over at him, pride in her eyes. "We weren't rich by any means, but we had each other. There was always love in the home."

"How did you meet your late husband?" Auggie wanted to know what kind of a man Steven Hamilton had been. "If it causes you pain to talk about him, I understand."

"The pain of losing him is fading being replaced by the memories." Elizabeth looked at him a small smile on her face. "Steven was the son of a farmer down the road from us. We grew up with each other, going to school and church and such things as that. Many thought we would naturally marry one day. I scuffed at such things.

"But it took some work on his part to convince me what others saw," Elizabeth smiled again, this time with a small sparkle in her eyes. "He kept having reasons for me to mend his work clothes until one day he asked me to a barn raising for another local farmer. I only said yes hoping that he'd stop pestering me, and next thing I knew we were married and in a wagon heading here."

Auggie sat quietly watching passion light up her face. She truly loved her husband. How did one compete with that kind of love? He couldn't, but he was going to find a way.

"So, you were happy after all?" Auggie smiled, pulling out the sandwiches and cheese. "That's good. So many couples marry for reasons other than love."

"Yes, we were happy and very much in love." Elizabeth smiled, scooping up a piece of cheese. "And what about you Auggie? Has there been any one special in your life?"

"At one time I thought there may have been, but not anymore." Auggie answered his nerves on edge. "Things didn't work out as my family had hoped they would."

"Oh, what happened?" Elizabeth asked, sipping her tea.

"When I took the opportunity to build the Grand, the plans my parents once had for me were gone." He was hedging. Avoiding the real reason he'd built the Grand. That he ran away from the past hoping to find a fresh start where no one knew him or his family. Coupled with the fact that she came from a humble background while he had been living high off the hog his entire life. But things were different now. He was a self-made man who lived modestly but comfortable enough.

But was it enough for a wife and family?

"YOU'RE A SUCCESSFUL man, Auggie. I'm sure your parents are proud of you." Elizabeth meant every word. She was surprised to feel that they came from her heart. He was so much more than he thought he was.

"Yes, well..." Auggie bit into a sandwich looking away from her.

Whatever he was ashamed of she couldn't imagine. Augustine Raines was the finest man she'd met since Steven. And if things were different...

What am I thinking! Things aren't different. I'm a widow with no intention of ever falling in love again. Never marrying a man again. One heartbreak a lifetime is enough for anyone. Besides, he's never acted like he was interested in more than friendship. Which suits me just fine.

"You said you grew up on a horse ranch. What kind of horses did you have?" Elizabeth asked slipping another piece of cheese in her mouth.

"Mostly Thoroughbreds," Auggie answered swallowing. "Father bred horses for the track. It was the only way mother would allow any kind of gambling.

"Betting on a good breeding season was as close to the track as father ever came, that mother knows of anyway." Auggie chuckled. "I don't know how many times I was sworn to secrecy as a child. If one of our horses were running, father would take me to the track. He loved to watch them run—and win."

"And did they win often?" Elizabeth asked smiling along with him. Evidently men like to keep secrets from their wives. *Did Steven ever keep any from her?* She wondered frowning a bit.

"Elizabeth, is something wrong?"

"No, I was just thinking of the secrets men keep from their wives. And wondering if—" Elizabeth began feeling an ache in her heart at the possibility.

"If Steven had kept any from you?"

"Yes." She looked up at him willing the tears away. "But then I remember how much we loved each other. How gentle and kind he was. I know he would have never kept anything from me that was important. And if he did it was only to protect me."

"I'm sure you are correct in that assumption." Auggie reassured her. "And if he had you can bet Willa would have known it and done something about it!"

Elizabeth laughed out loud. "Oh my, yes she would have. Thank you Auggie for reminding me.

"Now we were talking about your life on the ranch. What made you leave it all behind?"

"I lost interest in horses and couldn't see my life as my father had wanted."

Auggie wouldn't make eye contact with her and in that moment she knew something was wrong. Had something happened to one of the horses and it was his fault? She didn't think he wasn't telling the truth, just avoiding it as much as possible.

Elizabeth wondered what could have been so horrible that a person would lie about it.

"Well, I'm not sure if I would have lost interest. They are beautiful." Elizabeth smiled looking at the carriage horses happily grazing on blades of grass.

"And dangerous," Auggie replied gathering up their picnic dinner. "I think we'd better get back."

"Okay," Elizabeth said helping to pack the basket.

She took Auggie's hand, bumping into him as she stood. His arm around her waist he held her close. Close enough to feel his heart beating. Close enough to smell him. Close enough that if she looked up he could kiss her.

"Steady now," he said releasing her.

"Thank you," Elizabeth stepped away feeling a loss of something that could have been. What that was she couldn't imagine.

They placed the basket and blanket into the back of carriage and rode back into Blessings Valley without saying more than a "good-night" when he dropped her off at her door.

CHAPTER 17

A few weeks later

Auggie stood on the small plot of land where the Grand garden would go, watching the landscapers prepare for the plants that were due any day now. Between Elizabeth and himself, they'd finally agreed upon the type of lawn furniture and plants. The gazebo was already built and sat in the middle of the garden, waiting like a lady for her beau. Or a tea party between friends to chat about the latest town gossip.

"How's it coming along, Auggie?"

Auggie smiled and turned toward the voice he'd come to love. Love? The single word popped up in his mind on more occasions then he cared to admit. It always did whenever Elizabeth was near or in his thoughts.

"Look for yourself, Elizabeth." Reaching for her hand, he helped her down the makeshift steps and onto the grounds. "If all goes well, I believe we should be ready by the end of the week to open it to everyone in Blessings Valley."

"It is going to be lovely, Auggie." Elizabeth smiled, strolling toward the gazebo.

Auggie walked alongside her, thinking how lovely she looked. She had on a late summer dress, her hair fell softly around her shoulders, and the smile on her face was sunny. Just like her. A ray of sunshine.

"So, you approve?" Auggie asked, wanting badly to pull her into his arms. It had been several weeks since their picnic dinner, and he missed those few hours of intimacy between them. Once the work on the garden had started there hadn't been time to ask her to dinner again. But there will be in the future, if he played his cards right.

"Do I approve?! What a silly question, Auggie." Elizabeth laughed, walking around the inside perimeter of the gazebo. "This is so perfect and once the benches and tables arrive, well, let's just say I'm looking forward to having lunch out here."

"I think that can be arranged," Auggie said. "I know the owner of this establishment and have some influence over the cook as well."

"Hmmm, throwing your weight around, are you?" Elizabeth smiled, standing in front of him.

Why don't I just say the hell with what people think and take her in my arms? No one would see us back here. No one but the workers that is.

"Not in the least," Auggie replied, keeping his thoughts, and his hands, to himself.

"What are you going to do with yourself once this is done, Auggie?" Elizabeth asked, stepping off the floor of the shelter toward the hotel.

"I do have an idea on how to expand the front of the hotel." Auggie walked slowly alongside her, his hands folded behind his back. "There is room on the other side of the steps that could be used for—something."

"Something? You don't have any plans yet?" Elizabeth asked, her eyes lighting up with curiosity. "There are so many possibilities."

"I have been considering something but nothing solid just yet. I've been consulting with some builders, that's why you've seen them outside the front window." Auggie smiled. He knew what he had planned and in time he would reveal it to her. But not until it was finished, if he was able to keep the secret from her.

"That's a good space and I'm sure you'll come up with something," Elizabeth said taking his hand as he assisted her back inside. "Do you think this doorway should be widened a bit? To accommodate entering the garden?"

"I have given some thought of building a smoking lounge for the gentlemen," Auggie replied as they walked through the dining room toward her sewing room. "I think there may be enough room for a small porch and wide steps down into the garden." "What do you think? Good idea or a bad one?"

"I think a good one. It will give those who don't wish to walk the garden a chance to sit outside, sip some tea, and still enjoy its beauty."

Elizabeth pushed open the door to her sewing room, then turned toward him. "Was there anything else, Auggie?"

Auggie swallowed desperately searching his mind for anything tangible. Coming up with nothing, he felt like a balloon that had just lost its air. Deflated. "No, that was all. Thank you Elizabeth."

"Of course, that's what you've asked me to do isn't it? Help you with the garden?" Smiling, she walked into the room and closed the door behind her.

"Blast!" Auggie swore under his breath, staring at the barrier between them.

ELIZABETH STOOD BEHIND the closed door waiting to see if he'd knock. When he didn't all hope seem to evaporate from her. They'd been alone in the garden. He could have taken that opportunity to at least hold her hand. But he hadn't.

Was she wishing for too much? Was this her punishment for finding herself attracted to another man less than a year after her late husband's death?

"No, I won't believe it," Elizabeth whispered finally stepping away from the door. "He likes me. I like him. A lot."

Picking up her recent mending, Elizabeth gazed out the small window. Would she and Auggie be one of those couples to stroll among the flowers of the garden? Not as employer and employee, but as, well, a couple in the early stages of courting? Friends learning that their friendship had blossomed into something more?

They'd sit under the gazebo quietly chatting about their day. How busy the hotel had been. How her mending was piling up as they gazed into each other's eyes. They'd eat the small sandwiches Mary had made for them and sip the cold sweet tea.

But that was a daydream. One that wouldn't ever happen because she was a widow who still loved her late husband. He was a man who came from prime racing stock, not dirt-poor farmland like her.

They were as different as night and day. Oil and water. Definitely not like a needle and thread that were meant to be together sewing two pieces of fabric together until there was only one.

Still, her heart wouldn't let the hope go. Not yet anyway.

Knock, knock

Elizabeth sucked in a breath. Could it be Auggie had come back after all?

She put her mending into the basket, straightened her skirt and said, "Come in!"

The door swung open. Elizabeth's hopeful heart gave way to disappointment. In the doorway stood Willa a smile on her face and a tray of food in her hands.

"I come with bribes" she said placing the tray on the table.

"Bribes for what?" Elizabeth asked harnessing in her disappointment that it had been Willa and not Auggie to walk in.

"Why all the building that is going on, that's what!" Willa exclaimed taking a seat across the table from Elizabeth.

"Willa! I didn't think you were prone to gossip," Elizabeth teased sipping the cool sweet tea.

"You wound me Elizabeth." Willa pouted for a moment then smiled. "That's why I've come straight to you where I know the information is not idle chitchat gossip."

"If you must know, Auggie is putting in a garden in the back just off from the dining room." Elizabeth said spreading jam on a piece of toast. "We've been planning it for several weeks and finally agreed on landscaping and furniture."

"That is wonderful, but what about the front of the hotel? There seems to be a lot of activity surrounding that space," Willa said, her gaze firmly on Elizabeth.

"That I can't help you with. He hasn't asked me to help him with it." Elizabeth bit into the toast, the sweet jam sliding down her throat. "Mary makes the best jam. It's smooth as silk. Sweet but not too."

"Come on, Elizabeth, you must know something," Willa insisted, looking at her over the rim of the glass.

"All I know is that it is a place for the gentlemen to go now that the garden is near completion. And I've been banned from the area." Elizabeth pouted. "It's like he thinks I don't know what men would like in a space of their own."

"Well, do you?" Willa asked.

"Of course not!" Elizabeth laughed.

"How have the two of you been getting along? Any more picnics?" Willa winked.

"I would like to believe that we are friends," Elizabeth answered, playing with the fruit on her plate. "We have both been too busy to plan picnics. We are lucky to eat lunch during the day. It's rare, like today had been. We had a few moments to walk through the garden. In fact, I thought it had been Auggie knocking." She said with a tinge of disappointment coming through her words.

"Would you like it to be more than friends?" Willa put her glass down.

"I'm not sure. Steven hasn't been gone a year yet." Elizabeth looked up with tears welling in her eyes. "I enjoy his company and he makes me feel, well, important. Like I may have a place with him in his life."

"You mean besides working here?" Willa suggested.

"Yes." Elizabeth nodded. "It is too soon, isn't it? Would I be betraying Steven if I, if I had started to develop a fondness of Auggie?"

"Depends." Willa answered her eyebrows raised. "Have you?"

"I think so." Elizabeth smiled her heart leapt as the knowledge of her words hung in the air.

AUGGIE STOOD ON the front step of the hotel going over the plans for the dress shop in his head. He planned on surprising Elizabeth with.

"Have some tea, Auggie," Mary's voice flowed into his thoughts.

He looked down at Mary, taking the sweating glass from her. "Did I see Willa come in not long ago?"

"You did." Mary confirmed. "She came to surprise Elizabeth during lunch. It has been a while since the two of them have talked."

"Hmm," Auggie mused wondering what their two benefactors were up to this time around. "And the reason for your visit, Mary?"

"Oh, just thought you'd like some tea." Mary said grinning like a cat eyeing a mouse.

"Come now, you know I've known you too long to believe that one." Auggie chuckled shaking his head.

"All right then," Mary huffed under her breath. "What do you plan to do about Elizabeth?"

Auggie was stunned. "What do you mean? Has something happened?"

"You know perfectly well what I mean, Augustine." Mary said grabbing the sleeve of his coat. "I'm not blind. I've see the way you look at her."

"Don't be absurd. We are friends, Mary. Not to mention I am her employer." Auggie protested a bit too strongly. He wasn't ready to admit anything to anyone, not even himself. And when he did, well, he'd cross that path when the time came.

"Oh fiddle sticks! I think you are just a bit more than friends. You'd know it too if you were honest with yourself." Mary scolded taking a firm hold of his arm.

"Mary, I don't think—"

"That's the problem, Auggie." Mary's voice was softer now and motherly love sparkled in her eyes. "I have been watching the two of you out in the garden. If you could see what I see you'd be saying the same thing. You are in love with Elizabeth, Auggie!"

Horrified, Auggie looked around making sure no one heard what Mary had said.

"Let's continue this conversation in my office, Mary." Auggie said, taking her arm and escorting her through the lobby and into his office. Privacy was needed for this conversation.

"Please do sit down." Auggie motioned as he sat across his desk from her.

"What do you plan to do about it?" Mary demanded, arms crossed over her chest.

Auggie sat back taking a deep breath. "What can I do, Mary? Elizabeth hasn't been widowed a year yet. She is still mourning the loss of her husband."

"Are you sure about that?" Mary asked, her brows raised in speculation.

"As sure as any man can be." Auggie said wishing everything Mary said were true. He did have feelings for Elizabeth, that much was certain. "Even if what you wish for were true, there's the issue of my disfiguring accident. Once she sees my face she'll turn and run the other way."

"For pity sake! Give her more credit than that," Mary spat shaking her head. "And when will you stop using that silly accident as an excuse?"

"I do give her more credit than you think, Mary." Auggie smiled remembering how she came into the office demanding him to explain her added workload. "She's strong and determined. And her smile is stunning when something makes her happy. And her eyes—"

Auggie glanced over at Mary finally seeing the knowing smile on her face. "What?"

"I knew it!" Mary rejoiced. "You'd better do something and soon, Auggie. Before it's too late."

"I have a plan, Mary," Auggie admitted praying she'd keep his secret.

"I bet it has nothing to do with the garden and everything to do with the 'smoking room.'" Mary grinned.

"How did you know?" Auggie felt sweat bead upon his brow.

"I saw that plan right there out in the open when we walked in," she said, pointing to the draft blueprint of the dress shop on his desk laying open for all the world to see.

CHAPTER 18

"What did you find out?" Willa asked as she returned the tray to the kitchen.

"Most likely the same thing you did," Mary answered a smile upon her face. "He loves her."

"And she him, I'm certain." Willa smiled back. "Now, what do we do about it?"

"I think I've put a few thoughts into his head. He's building that 'smoking room' for the gentlemen, so he says," Mary began.

"But you think it's for Elizabeth?" Willa asked. "I thought the garden was for her, not the expansion."

"I think you are wrong." Mary moved in closer to Willa, then took a peek down the hallway before closing the door. "I saw the blueprints on his desk," she said, lowering her voice.

"And?" Willa raised her eyebrows hoping her friend didn't take forever in coming forth with her information.

"I didn't know a smoking room had both a dressing room and a sewing room!" Mary said, poking Willa in the arm.

"Then he has plans for her!" Willa clapped down her excitement.

"From what I saw, I would say he does," Mary agreed, pulling a sack of flour from a shelf.

"Then our work here is about done." Willa smiled, placing the soiled dishes from the tray into the sink.

"BLAST!" AUGGIE SWORE not caring who did or did not hear him.

He'd never anticipated anyone see the blueprints for the expansion. He'd been careless when he left his office to check on the materials by leaving them out in the open on top of the desk.

What was done was done. He could trust Mary not to say anything.

Sitting back in the chair, he ran his fingers through his beard. Even though he kept it neatly trimmed, he could barely feel the outline of his jaw anymore.

Was Mary correct in that he needed to step from the wall he'd been hiding behind?

"I'm only hiding the scar, not myself," he mused shaking his head trying to convince himself his words were true. He hadn't seen his face in such a long time. At least not what lay underneath the wiry hair he used as a crutch.

Pushing away from his desk, Auggie tucked the blueprints under his arm and walked out into the lobby.

"Stewart, I'll be in my apartment if you need me." Auggie nodded to his desk clerk then sprinted up the staircase taking the steps two at a time.

Bursting into his apartment, he tossed the blueprints on to the table and draped his jacket over a chair before walking into his bedroom.

Auggie found himself in front of the mirror above the washbasin, a lathered shaving brush in his hand and droplets of water plopping into the water. To some men, shaving was a daily occurrence. But to him his beard was a wall that he hid behind. Was he really ready to expose himself again?

He stared down at the brush in his hand. His heart pounded against his chest in anticipation.

If he was to expect Elizabeth to give all of herself to him, it was only fair that he gave all of himself. Scars heal a lot quicker on the surface than the pain that caused it on your soul. Especially when a person hides behind that pain like he had been for years.

Like Mary said, it was time for him to stop hiding. It was time for him to own up to the man that he'd become, scars and all.

"Here goes." Auggie swirled the lathered brush around his face until his beard was completely covered with the shaving soap.

Picking up the blade, he watched as each short, crisp stroke peeled away the barrier on his face. He shut out the scraping sound of the blade against his skin. He shut out the scar as it slowly became uncovered.

Closing his eyes, Auggie splashed water on his face removing any soap and hair residue, before he towel-dried his moist skin. Avoiding the mirror, he emptied the bowl and cleaned off his razor before putting his shaving kit away.

Slipping back into his dress shirt and jacket, Auggie adjusted the clothing. It was a stall tactic, pure and simple.

"Get on with it, Raines!" he admonished himself. "Best you see first what everyone else is going to see. Then at least you'll know how to deal with the looks of disgust."

Gaze down, he walked slowly over to the mirror. He looked up slowly and smiled.

The ugly, swollen, red scar he remembered had faded. The thing he'd feared all these years was nothing more than a memory.

He'd forgotten how much he looked like his father. He had his mother's eyes, but the line of his face was all his father. And to his surprise, he found he liked the way he looked. Liked it very much.

Would Elizabeth?

ELIZABETH STOOD AT the window watching as more timber was being delivered for the smoking room. Soon she'd lose her view of the street, not to mention the light that came in while she worked, once the window was closed off for good. Maybe she would make a suggestion to Auggie about enlarging the north window.

Maybe once the garden was done, she'd be able to take some of the mending out there. She could sit either under the gazebo or on the porch. There'd be plenty of light to work by and the scent of the flowering plants to enjoy.

But how could she manage on those rainy days when storm clouds filled the sky? Or during the winter months when the northern winds carried the cold on them? The lamp no doubt as it has already given light before when she worked into the dusk of the coming night.

For now, her worktable could be moved to the northern corner of the room and she could sit in front of the window there. The view wouldn't be of main street, but at least she'd have some natural light to work by.

All these changes would certainly depend on Auggie's finances once the renovations were completed. She hoped he wasn't overextending the hotel's accounts. For his sake as well as her own.

"A penny for your thoughts."

Auggie! Elizabeth's heart leapt. She turned, halting halfway.

"You shaved!" she exclaimed studying his face.

He looked younger than she thought him to be. The strong angle of his jawline curved toward a square, dimpled chin. He was more handsome then she could have ever imagined.

"You approve then?" Auggie's fingers travelled along his chin and she couldn't help but follow their path.

She walked over to him to get a closer look. "Oh yes!" she said, feeling her smile fill her face.

"And the scar, it doesn't offend you?" He took several steps closer to her, so close that she could smell his faint manly scent.

"The scar?" she asked looking again as he turned his face to the left. "I hadn't noticed until you told me it was there."

"It's not hideous to you?" He asked sounding a bit nervous.

"No! Why should it?" she asked, not quite understanding his concern about an old injury.

"I always thought it was horrible." He confessed turning back to face her.

"We all have scars, Auggie. Some of them you just can't see." Elizabeth knew where her scar lay— deep in her heart. "How did you get it?"

"A bet made by a very stupid young man," Auggie looked at her embarrassment in his eyes.

"I can't imagine that young man being anything close to stupid," Elizabeth said, touching his arm. "Especially if that young man was the man standing before me now. One who is strong and confident. Who knows who he is. What he wants. Yet also kind and compassionate toward others."

"Well, I was. Thought I had something to prove to my friends on my new mount." Auggie ironically laughed. "Instead of winning the race, I ended up against one of the old oak trees on our property. My face was sliced open and blood everywhere. Once I could, I grew the beard to hide the deformity, as well as my shame."

"Don't be silly. I think it adds character to your face." Elizabeth stood on her toes and on impulse lightly kissed the scar.

CHAPTER 19

"Elizabeth," he whispered. Hugging her, he pulled her close. She'd kissed him, or rather his scar. And even though it was a sweet, innocent kiss it was a kiss nonetheless "Thank you for that."

Elizabeth looked up at him a small smile on her face. "I meant every word, Auggie."

"Yes, well…" Auggie started fighting back the doubt threatening to surface. "That's not the entire story though, Elizabeth. You may change your opinion of me after you hear the truth."

Releasing her, his heart immediately felt her absence. The feeling, while not new to him since she'd come into his life, intensified the longer his arms were absent of her. The only time he'd held her that close had been the one time when they'd danced, and even then they'd been under the watchful eye of Mary and Willa.

"I'm a coward, Elizabeth," Auggie confessed. Hands stuffed deep into his pant pockets, he strolled over to the window and watched the construction for the 'gentlemen's smoking lounge' take place just outside. Another lie he'd have to come clean about soon.

Mustering courage, he turned around to find Elizabeth watching and waiting. There was no pity in her eyes, only compassion; it was all the courage he needed. "I grew the beard to hide behind. Then I came here to keep from having to suffer rejection from any women I met or already knew. I felt I couldn't stay home any longer because everyone there knew of the racing bet and the accident resulting from it. I didn't want their pity. I didn't want to know they only tolerated my being at their side because of who my family is."

Elizabeth stepped over to him and lightly traced the scar with the tip of her finger. He didn't feel her recoil from it. He didn't feel anything but the soft, gentle caress of her soft skin against his smooth face.

"To know you, really know you, is to know all of you," Elizabeth said, her touch lingering a moment longer.

"Is that what you'd like, Elizabeth? To get to know all of me?" Auggie asked, hope rising to new levels in his heart.

"I think so, Auggie." Elizabeth smiled at him.

"Good, because that's all I've wanted for months now." Taking her in his arms once again, he kissed her gently on the lips.

When she returned the kiss, he felt her melt in his arms. Her heart beat as fast as his as their kiss deepened. He felt...he wasn't sure what else he felt except happiness. Anything beyond that was premature and the thoughts that came with it disrespectful towards Elizabeth, who deserved nothing but to be highly respected.

"Mr. Raines?" Stewart's voice followed the knock upon the sewing room door.

Auggie froze for a moment before unwrapping himself from around Elizabeth. Waiting for a discreet moment while she righted herself, he pulled open the door.

"Yes, Stewart, what is it?"

"The train has arrived with a rather large shipment for the hotel on it," Stewart informed, a knowing grin on his face, handing Auggie the shipping notice.

"Thank you. Have a wagon brought around and we'll go see what has arrived," Auggie instructed.

Stewart nodded then dashed through the dining room to do as Auggie had asked.

"Do you think it's the lawn furniture?" Elizabeth asked looking as if nothing had happened between them.

"I certainly hope so." Auggie stepped next to her, sliding his hands gently over her arms. "Do you wish to come along with me?"

"No, I think I'll stay here and work on some mending." Elizabeth returned to her table and picked up a jacket she'd been working on.

"Elizabeth—" Auggie felt that he should be apologizing for kissing her without permission to do so.

"Go, Auggie!" Elizabeth said, her smile bright. "I can take care of myself well enough."

"Only if you promise that we will talk about the, what happened a moment ago later," Auggie compromised. "I'll escort you home tonight, if you'll allow me."

"I'd like that, Auggie." Elizabeth grinned, her eyes sparkling like blue sapphires.

Auggie nodded then walked briskly through the dining room whistling.

"WHAT HAVE I done?" Tears welling in her eyes, Elizabeth plopped down in the chair. The jacket crumpled in her lap, her fingers trembling. "For a second, no, a third time, I let another man kiss me. Worse, I kissed him back! I've betrayed my Steven's memory."

Elizabeth, don't be silly. You didn't betray anyone. Auggie is a nice man, an honest man.

"But I made a promise to always love you, only you, Steven." She said, wiping tears from her eyes. Guilt riddling her mind.

And I always will be somewhere in your heart. Find room for another, Elizabeth.

"There isn't enough room anymore for anyone else. My heart was always yours and always will be."

You must open it to another. You can't live your life alone, you've too much to live for. You know you like Auggie, don't you?

"Yes, but—"

I won't hear of it. Promise that you'll open your heart to more than a friendship. That you'll find someone to love again. Someone like Auggie Raines.

"I promise."

I will always be in your heart, if you need me, Elizabeth. Auggie may be the one to be here to hold you. To cherish you. To love you for the rest of your days. It doesn't mean you loved me any less.

"I know."

Elizabeth heard the wagon pull up outside her window. Jumping up from the chair, she looked out in time to see Auggie climb aboard. Turning she ran out the door, through the dining room and out the front door.

"Auggie!" she called out as the wagon began to pull away. She wasn't sure if she was relieved or sadden when the wagon kept moving toward the station. Or disappointed that Auggie hadn't heard her.

"Elizabeth, is everything all right? I saw you running through the lobby," Mary asked concern on her face.

"Yes. No," Elizabeth said, doing her best to hold back to the tears.

"Looks to me like you could use a cup of tea." Mary suggested squeezing Elizabeth's elbow. "Come on to the kitchen. I just took some German coffee bread out of the oven."

"Oh, I couldn't Mary," Elizabeth said, turning to go back into the hotel. "I have several pieces that need mending, and—"

"Of course, you can! And the mending can wait for a few minutes," Mary insisted guiding Elizabeth back to the kitchen.

Mary put the tea kettle on, then sliced a few pieces of the warm bread. "Tell me what has you so upset. Did Auggie do something?"

"Yes," Elizabeth answered, her mind searching for a way to say what happened without sounding like a gold-digging widow.

"I will skin that boy alive!" Mary said placing the plate on the table with a clank. "Sorry. He was raised better than that. What has he done?"

Elizabeth looked up at Mary worrying her bottom lip. How could she tell her that she kissed Auggie? Not once but twice!

"Did you know that Auggie shaved this morning?" Elizabeth began, hoping to avoid anything having to do with their kissing.

Mary stopped pouring the hot water. "He did what?" she exclaimed, sitting down at the table with wonderment on her face. "Did you say he …"

"He shaved off his beard." Elizabeth sighed smiling despite herself. "He has a rather handsome face. And he looks years younger."

"And the scar?" Mary asked.

"The scar?" Elizabeth was confused. What would his scar have to do with the way he looks?

"You don't find it hideous?" Mary asked, concern etched across her face.

"Quite the opposite." Elizabeth felt heat rise in her cheeks. "I find it quite appealing. It adds character to his features."

"Did you tell him that?" Mary asked.

"Well, not in so many words. I kissed it," Elizabeth gushed. "The scar, I kissed the scar." She looked at Mary waiting for a sign that she'd made the biggest mistake of her life.

"You kissed Auggie?" Mary asked, grinning.

"In a way. I kissed his scar." Elizabeth sighed, lowering her eyes. She wouldn't be able to stand to see the shame that was sure to be in Mary's eyes. "Then he kissed me."

"And?" Mary asked.

"I kissed him back." Elizabeth wiped tears from her eyes. "I don't know what came over me, Mary. After he left to go to the station I thought I'd done something horrible. Betrayed Steven's memory. Then I realized that Auggie is a nice man and that I, well I find that I like him very much."

"So why were you running through the lobby?" Mary asked her hands folded calmly in front of her a grin on her face.

"To go with him to the station. He'd asked and I'd said no because I was embarrassed." Elizabeth confessed.

"And you aren't embarrassed any longer?" Mary grinned, sipping from her teacup.

"Not at all." Elizabeth smiled feeling the weight of bricks lifting from her.

"THAT SHOULD BE everything, Stewart." Auggie said glancing at the load in the wagon before climbing back aboard. "Please bring the crates marked *Singer Manufacturing Company* directly to my office. Everything else can be unloaded and uncrated in the garden after that."

He hadn't expected the sewing machine to arrive with the rest of the cargo. Hopefully, Stewart could get it secured in Auggie's office before Elizabeth found out they were back.

"Does this mean the garden will be ready

soon?" Stewart asked.

"I'm sure if Mrs. Hamilton has anything to say about it, it will be ready by the morning light." Auggie chuckled knowing full well once they pulled in behind the hotel, Elizabeth would be anxious to get the crates unpacked and ordering them where to place everything.

"Then I will make sure there is plenty of help," Stewart offered. Snapping the reins, he called out, "Walk on."

"Just make sure both of those crates get into my office without Mrs. Hamilton seeing them," Auggie reiterated again.

During the short ride back to the hotel Auggie's mind floated back to the kiss he'd shared with Elizabeth. But that wasn't what weighed heavily on his mind. Had it been a mistake to shave his beard? If not for Stewart's interruption he may have found out if it was or wasn't. Even if it hadn't seemed like it was, he couldn't help but doubt. Elizabeth was to kind to say anything awful about his disfigurement, at least not to his face.

Lord please see it in your mercy that Elizabeth has not been offended by my looks. That she is still there waiting for my return. She needs us, as much as we all need her.

"I take it Mrs. Hamilton doesn't know about the addition to the sewing room?" Stewart asked interrupting before Auggie could think *amen.*

"Amen," he said under his breath instead.

"Then it will be interesting when she finds out. Do you think she'll be pleased?" Stewart asked unaware of the real reason for the *Singer.*

"I certainly do hope so," Auggie nodded. "Be sure to go around to the back. It'll be easier to unload, then uncrate, everything."

Steward nodded as he drove between the empty sheriff's office and the Grand. "When does the new sheriff arrive in town?"

"I haven't heard. I almost thought he'd be on the train since he's coming from New York City," Auggie answered, not having given the arrival of Owen Rawlins much thought. It had been less than a month since Blessings Valley had been without law and order, and they'd fared rather well without it. But everyone knew that was something that wouldn't last without a sheriff in town.

"This is good, Stewart," Auggie said as they came to the back entrance to the garden. "I'll go and delay Mrs. Hamilton as much as possible while you and the boys get those special crates in my office." Auggie jumped down from the wagon and sprinted up the porch steps then through the dining room.

Catching his breath, he knocked at the sewing room door and waited until the door opened.

"Auggie!" Elizabeth said, a smile on her face. "Was that the shipment for the garden?"

"Yes, it was. Let's give the men a chance to uncrate everything before you instruct them were to put the furniture," Auggie said, relieved that she didn't appear to be upset with him.

"And it will give us a chance to talk about..." she began, her gaze sweeping back down to the floor.

"The scar," he finished for her.

"The scar?" she asked, confusion in her eyes.

"Yes, this disfigurement," he said, pointing to the place where the skin along his jaw was only a slightly different color from the rest of his face. "Now that you've had time to consider your initial comments, I'm sure you realize how hideous it makes me look."

"Is that what you think of yourself? Of me? That I would take back words I meant with every ounce of my being?" Elizabeth gaped at him, her eyes filling with sadness. "I thought you had come to know me better than that, Auggie."

She turned from him, and his heart cracked. Reaching for her, she slipped out of his fingers.

"You really aren't offended?" Auggie asked, taking a careful step toward her.

"No, Auggie, I am not offended. How could I be when I am very fond of you, with or without a scar on your face. That scar doesn't change who you are by any means." She turned, her gazed fixed on his.

"And the kisses? What about the kisses?" Auggie asked, feeling like a silly schoolboy once again.

"I have to admit, at first I felt guilty. Thought I was betraying my late husband," Elizabeth admitted, her gaze somewhere Auggie didn't belong. But then she looked at him and he felt he was exactly where he belonged...with her. "Then I realized that Steven will always have a place in my heart. And that there is room for someone who has already found his way into it."

Auggie placed his hands on her arms and searched her eyes for any trace of pity or lies.

Again, he found none.

"And you have found a way into mine as well, Elizabeth," Auggie whispered, pulling her into his arms. When she looked up at him, he captured her mouth with his before tearing himself away from her.

"Let's go see if things are uncrated." He smiled, then captured her hand in his.

CHAPTER 20

Late Summer

"You've done wonderfully with the garden, Elizabeth." Willa praised, strolling through the grounds. "I can see why you long to spend time out here."

"Thank you. It was all Auggie though." Elizabeth blushed, her heart swelling with pride and growing love. "He came up with the idea for a place where a lady could sit in quiet to read, have a cup of tea, think, or even spend time with someone special."

"Is that what Auggie has been doing out here?" Willa asked smiling at her. "Spending time with someone special?"

"I'm not sure what you are getting at, Willa." Elizabeth sighed wishing she could confirm Auggie's intentions. But she wasn't sure what they were. They were friends and had become closer.

MAXINE DOUGLAS

Anything more than that on his part was a mystery to her. She on the other hand found she'd grown fond of him, very fond.

"Auggie has been extremely busy with the gentlemen's smoking lounge. I've been spending as much time as possible out here working on the mending once the window had been blocked off several days ago. Today is the first day I've been able to enjoy the beauty of the garden without a needle and thread in my hand."

"So you don't spend any time together out here at all?" Willa asked surprise in her voice.

"We have had lunch on the porch once or twice since the construction has slowed down." Elizabeth didn't want to talk about her relationship with Auggie. At least not until there was something of importance to discuss. Looking toward the garden porch, she found the distraction she'd hoped for. "Oh look, there's Mary!"

Elizabeth hurried over to take the tray from Mary, thankful for her timely appearance. She wasn't ready to talk about Auggie and her relationship, or lack of it with Willa, or anyone for that matter.

"Mary, let me take that from you." Elizabeth reached for the tray, relieving it from Mary's grasp.

"Thank you, Elizabeth. I wasn't sure I'd make it all the way to the gazebo or not." Mary nervously laughed. "I didn't think it would be that heavy in so short of a walk. Guess I'm not that spring chicken I used to be."

"You aren't getting old Mary, just wise. But you should have had Stewart or one of the others help you." Elizabeth said concerned that Mary sometimes did more than she should. "If you had taken a tumble down those steps, Auggie would never have forgiven me."

"You all worry too much. I love you for it, but you need not be concerned about me." Mary protested. "I see Willa is already here. Has she been grilling you about Auggie?"

"Oh, you know Willa." Elizabeth giggled. "Of course she has!"

"Hello Mary," Willa called waving from the gazebo.

Reaching the gazebo, Elizabeth set the tray down as Mary greeted Willa with a hug. "Smells like corned beef sandwiches, Mary."

"It is along with southern corn and some fruit. I thought to keep it light but filling." Mary beamed as she took a seat close to Willa. "And some tea. Wish I could have made some lemonade but the hotel pantry is out of fresh lemons."

As the dishes were passed around and the tea poured, one-by-one they filled their plates with meat, bread, corn and fruit.

"How are things at the boardinghouse, Willa?" Mary asked sipping from the tea. "It has been quiet here at the hotel, I imagine the same is for you."

"I've been holding my own, but yes the boardinghouse is not full." Willa answered spreading butter over her bread. "I recently received a telegram from an attorney requesting a room for a Mr. Wallace Baldwin, arrival date unknown. Do you think it could be any relation to Vera's late husband, Elizabeth?"

"I'm not sure. Neither Vera nor Thomas ever talked much about their families." Elizabeth popped a slice of pear in her mouth, savoring the sweetness. "Oh my, these are wonderful. I never knew grilled pears could be so delicious."

"I wonder what business this Mr. Baldwin has in Blessings Valley then. The telegram was rather vague." Willa continued, ignoring Elizabeth's attempt to take the conversation on a different path. "I don't like vague and I don't like surprises. I like trouble even less."

"Willa, I'm surprised at you!" Mary exclaimed, putting her fork down with a clang. "Since when did you subject yourself to idle gossip before you know what the truth is?"

"I am only curious, Mary." Willa defended herself and her question. "If I'm to hold a room for someone with no arrival date, well, it could be costly."

"That's simple, just charge extra for the room if you have to turn someone away." Elizabeth said simply. "Until this Mr. Wallace Baldwin arrives, you have no way of knowing whether or not you'll even be in need of that room."

"And if you are, just send them over here to the Grand." Mary suggested.

"All right then," Willa huffed, "have it your way."

"Good now that that is settled, can we go back to having a nice friendly lunch?" Elizabeth asked as they continued to chat quietly about the garden and the flowers about to come into late bloom.

"Good work, men." Auggie stood in the newest addition to the Grand Hotel—a dress shop. At least he hoped it would be a dress shop once Elizabeth found out about his secret building. All that was left was to enlarge the north window in the former sewing room, make the window he'd closed off into a door leading into the dress shop and it would be finished.

His part would be finished. The rest would be up the Elizabeth.

"Do you think you can have it finished yet today?" Auggie asked the foreman he'd hired to oversee the construction.

"Yes sir, Mr. Raines," the foreman said walking across the room to him. "We'll have the window in and the door up by dinnertime."

"Excellent!" Auggie said nodding head. "I appreciate you and your men for getting this done so quickly."

"We welcomed the work, Mr. Raines." The foreman nodded then returned to oversee his crew.

So far everything had been going according to plan. Once he walked Elizabeth home, he'd come back and make any final touches.

Ha, like I know what is needed in a dress shop! Or where things like dress forms and bolts of fabric would go. Hopefully the shelves will be of help.

Auggie chuckled then walked back into the hotel.

"Stewart, everything going well?" Auggie asked as he stopped for a moment to check-in with the desk clerk.

"Yes, sir. Mrs. Hall and Mrs. Hamilton are in

the garden having lunch with Mrs. Alexander," Stewart said smiling, "if you're looking for them."

"Thank you," Auggie felt his face warm before he darted through the dining room and onto the porch overlooking the garden.

The joyous sound of laughter reached his ears, stopping him in his tracks.

Elizabeth sat at the table under the gazebo laughing with Mary and Willa. Her face looking younger with the stress of the day forgotten. He loved seeing her this happy. It made him realize how much he needed her in his life, and he'd do anything to keep her in it.

To keep her with him as he ran the hotel.

To keep her with him as they watched their children and then their grandchildren run and play in the garden.

To keep her with him as they grew old together.

To keep her—

"Auggie!" Elizabeth called out waving at him. "Come have lunch with us."

"I'll have breakfast, lunch, and dinner with you for as long as I am alive," he whispered under his breath as he waved back and made his way down the steps.

"There is plenty left over if you haven't had lunch yet, Auggie," Mary said, sliding closer to Willa so he could pull up the fourth chair.

"Corned beef?" he asked, setting the chair between Elizabeth and Mary.

"Yes, and southern corn with grilled pears." Mary beamed.

"My favorites." He winked, buttering a slice of bread then piling meat on it. "Is the tea still cold?"

"I believe so." Elizabeth poured him a tall glass, then topped off the rest of the glasses as well. "How's the smoking lounge coming?"

Auggie coughed on the bite he'd taken, swallowing hard he nodded his head. "It's coming along nicely. Elizabeth, you will be happy to know that the north window is being replaced today. Next time you report for work it should be in. I warn you, there may be some cleanup needed."

"Thank you so much!" Elizabeth clapped her hands together. "I'll be happy to sweep up the floor tomorrow as long as I have more light in the room. I do wish the north window had the street view though."

"Yes, I'm sure you do. We'll have to see about tomorrow though," he said, scooping a good helping of corn onto his plate. "I did say the next time you reported to work."

"Isn't that tomorrow?" Elizabeth asked, confusion on her face. "It's not the end of the week yet, and I have plenty of mending that people are waiting for."

"You let me handle that, okay?" Auggie continued eating his lunch as if nothing was amiss. The longer he sat at the table with the three fine ladies, the harder it was going to be for him to keep the charade up.

"Willa, would you mind helping me carry everything into the kitchen?" Mary asked, gathering up the bowls and soiled dishes. "Elizabeth believes I am incapable of doing it myself; afraid I'm going to get hurt or something."

"Are you serious?" Willa looked at Mary then jumped in her chair. "Ouch!"

"Come now," Mary said, taking the tray as she stood.

"For the love of ..." Willa mumbled, stacking the bowls one by one then gathering them in her arms.

"Those two!" Elizabeth exclaimed, laughing lightly. "It's a good thing they are friends with all the bickering they do back and forth with each other."

Auggie stood then chuckled. "Come on, let me walk you home."

"Only if you tell me how you plan to handle the customers who are waiting for their garments." Standing, Elizabeth smiled and took Auggie's elbow.

"It's quite simple really, I told them the sewing room was closed until the construction was complete," Auggie said, patting her hand lightly. "I know how much you want to make them happy, but they all agreed to wait a day or two."

"All right then," Elizabeth said, placing her hand over his.

Auggie had never felt more sure of himself and his plan than he was as they walked arm-in-arm through the street of Blessings Valley.

"ARE YOU SURE the customers don't mind waiting an extra couple of days?" Elizabeth hated to disappoint anyone waiting for their mending. She prayed no one had anything important to wear their item to.

"Yes," Auggie answered quietly. "I told anyone expecting something tomorrow that they would have it Monday. So really, it's only an extra day since you don't come in during the weekend."

"I hope it won't hurt business for you," she said, feeling guilt creep into her mind. Guilt over not finishing something on time. Her promise was everything to her.

"I'm positive it won't." Auggie chuckled. "You amaze me, Elizabeth."

"How is that?" She looked up at him, his gaze kind and tender, and something that could be mistaken for affection. Not the kind of affection a friend has for a friend. No, she thought it looked like the kind a man has for a woman he wanted to spend his life with.

"Never mind, you don't have to answer that." She stammered.

"But I want to." Auggie paused for a moment in front of the church. "I am very fond of you, Elizabeth."

His finger tipped her chin upward and she gazed directly into his face and his eyes.

"I, I'm very fond of you as well Auggie." She whispered her heart racing. *How fond am I? Fond enough to think of him as more than a friend? Maybe? Possible? Yes!*

"That's good to know, Elizabeth." He bent down closer.

His lips kissing the corners of her mouth sending butterflies stirring in her tummy. His hands gently cupped her face, and his body moved closer to hers. As close as a lover would be.

Her arms went around him and she accepted his nearness. Her heart burst with love. Love for a man who accepted her for who she was. A man who cared for her.

And she for him.

"Now, let me get you home before I do something my father would whip me for." Auggie released her and a shiver ran over her.

"Okay," was all she could say. The last thing she expected was to feel alive again. Alive in a way she hadn't felt for months.

As they approached her house porch, he leaned in and kissed her gently on the forehead.

She felt him dislodge her hand from his arm. "I'll see you Monday morning."

"Monday morning," she answered slowly walking up the steps and into her house where she sunk against the door.

Could Auggie Raines be in love with her? Really in love with her?

And was she in love with him?

Panic streaked through her. She flung open the door and ran down to the church. She stood for a moment gazing up at the cross above the door then walked quickly up the steps and through the door.

Sitting in the first pew, she bowed her head and folded her hands.

Dear Merciful Lord, I know that I haven't been Your obedient daughter for many months. I know that I blamed You for taking my beloved Steven from me. But I now realize that You always have a plan, and that Steven's time of Earth was done.

That You needed him. Please Lord, forgive my doubts and my fears. And help the other widows who are lost to find their way back to You. I trust in You, oh Lord, to lead me on the path You have chosen. In God's name, Amen.

Tears came to her eyes and Elizabeth felt a calmness she hadn't experienced since the mining accident.

EPILOGUE

Monday Morning

Auggie worked all weekend to be sure the new addition was exactly as he had envisioned it. With the help of Mary and Willa, he'd found the perfect place for the sewing machine, cutting table, and other notions Elizabeth would need.

Now if only this wouldn't blow up in his face, his world would be right just as it had been since Elizabeth first walked into his office looking for a job as a seamstress.

"Stewart be sure Mrs. Hamilton comes straight into my office the moment she arrives," he said and then sat behind his desk nervous as all get out.

He'd never proposed to a woman before. Never thought he would. But then Elizabeth walked into his office and from that moment on he knew his life would never be the same.

Would she accept him?

He was willing to take that chance for love. Her love.

Knock, knock.

"Morning Auggie." Elizabeth stood in the doorway, her eyes bright and her cheeks flushed. "Stewart said you wanted to see me right away."

Struggling to control his urges to jump up and take her in his arms, he cleared his throat.

"Yes, the smoking lounge is complete." He swallowed hard as his heart hammered against his ribs. "I thought you'd like to see it before you got started this morning."

"I'd would like that very much." Elizabeth smiled at him, excitement in her eyes.

"Then let's go," he came around the desk, slipping his hand into hers. "Don't' worry, it's still early and Stewart already suspects."

"All right," she answered.

When they reached the door to the new addition, he paused for a moment taking both her hands in his.

"I'm going to ask you to close your eyes and trust me. Can you do that?"

"Of course, I can. I trust you with my life, Auggie."

As SHE HEARD the door open, Elizabeth held her breath resisting the urge to peek.

"Okay, you can look now." Auggie announced.

"What?" Elizabeth gasped, her hand covering her mouth. "Auggie!"

"Welcome to your dress shop, Elizabeth. Now before you say anything hear me out. The Grand will only receive a commission of the sales for a short time until you are on your feet. Then all proceeds will be yours and yours alone."

"Oh Auggie!" She whispered, tears trailing down her cheeks. "You did all of this for me?

"Yes, because you deserve it."

Elizabeth walked around the room her hand running along the edge of the cutting table. "Is there a sewing machine?"

"That's the best part." Auggie beamed with pride. "That door right there used to be the window to the sewing room. Now it is part of the dress shop."

Elizabeth walked through the door. There she found set up in front of the north picture window, standing next to a dress form, a Singer sewing machine complete with cabinet stood.

She turned to Auggie, taking his hands in hers. "Thank you for the generous offer. But before I accept I want to get something straight."

"I thought you might."

"You must give me a business loan." She said, biting her lower lip. Would he agree to take a chance on her even though she didn't have a business background? "Or at the very least an investment loan and partnership."

"On one condition." Auggie said.

"What?" Elizabeth asked afraid of what he wanted. She didn't have a business plan. Nor did she have any start-up funds. All she had was her desire and determination.

"That you consider marrying me." Auggie blurted out. "I love you, Elizabeth."

"I think I love you also. I might consider your proposal if you asked me properly," Elizabeth said. "And only after the dress shop is paying for itself."

"Elizabeth Hamilton, I wouldn't have it any other way" Auggie said, bending down on one knee, taking her hands in his. "Would you do me the honor of becoming my wife, and business partner?"

"Yes!" Elizabeth said tears of happiness flowing down her cheeks as Auggie slipped an engagement ring on her finger.

THE END

Thank you for reading *Widows of Blessings Valley: Elizabeth*. I hope you will come along with Vera Baldwin on the path of her grief after losing her husband Thomas in the mining accident of 1892, and how she handles the unexpected visit from her brother-in-law, Wallace Baldwin.

Widows of Blessings Valley: Vera will be coming out in the Fall of 2019.

BONUS EXCERPT

Vera

Widows of Blessings Valley, Book 2

Recently widowed, laundress Vera Baldwin is pregnant and terrified at being alone.

Assigned to investigate the mining accident that killed several men in Blessings Valley, undercover agent, Jack Daniels is torn between duty and family when he learns Vera Baldwin is carrying his estranged brother's child.

Can two strangers with a broken heart find love for the sake of an unborn child?

CHAPTER 1

Late Summer 1892

As she did every day before going to the laundry, Vera Baldwin stood over the grave of her late husband, Thomas. Tenderly smoothing her hand over her swelling belly, she fought the tears threatening to fall. They came less and less, but on days like today, it was hard to fight them off.

"Soon Thomas everyone will know the precious gift you left behind. I want to keep it my secret for as long as I can," she said wiping away the tears with the back of her hand. "It is a comfort to know that I'll always have a piece of you to hold and love every day of my life.

"Thank you, my love." Kneeling, she placed a kiss on the marker with her hand. "I will love you always."

Standing, Vera blew one more kiss at her deceased husband's grave then turned and began walking toward Blessings Valley. Back to Nana's Laundry that was now her life as a laundress. It wasn't how she'd imagined it would be when she and Thomas had married only two years earlier.

Thomas, three years her senior, rode onto her father's ranch one winter day looking for work. After only a few months as a ranch hand, Vera knew her heart would belong to Thomas. And he felt the same way. So much so that he asked her to marry him after getting her father's reluctant permission.

So, on her twentieth birthday, as they stood on the front porch in front of her family and the local preacher, she became Mrs. Thomas Baldwin. Two years later they set out for the Oklahoma Territory and settled in Blessings Valley six months ago. In the space of only a few years, Vera had turned from a rancher's daughter into a miner's wife.

Now she was a widow on her own. But she had more than herself to care for. There was a baby on the way and before long she wouldn't be able to hide her secret under her clothes.

Maybe I could ask Elizabeth Hamilton to alter a few of my dresses. She'd keep my secret if I asked her, wouldn't she? At least until the time came when Vera felt like she wanted to share it with everyone. If she could hide away until the baby came, she would.

"Morning," Vera called out walking through the back door to Nana's.

"Morning, Vera," Mollie answered, placing a folded sheet into a basket marked for the boardinghouse. "This is ready to go back to the boardinghouse. Do you think you can manage?"

"Yes," Vera answered, laughing nervously. "Why do you ask?"

"Well, a woman in your condition," Mollie smiled winking at Vera.

"My condition?" Vera stammered, her heart skipping a beat. "Just because I'm a widow doesn't mean I can't carry a laundry basket anymore."

"Anything you say," Mollie laughed. "In the meantime, please take this over to the boardinghouse and pick up what Willa has that needs to be laundered."

Vera nodded, gathering the wicker basket in her arms then headed out the door and across the street. *Does Mollie suspect? How could she when I've been so careful not to draw attention to myself?*

Reaching the boardinghouse, she went back door where she knew Willa would in the kitchen this time of morning preparing breakfast. As she rounded the corner, her stomach revolted slightly as the rich smell of coffee assaulted her senses. Pausing for a moment, she sucked in a breath until her tummy settled down and the nausea passed.

When will this sickness stop, she wondered,

breathing deeply and slowly.

Feeling more settled, Vera knocked on the door once then pushed in. "Morning Willa," she said. Just as she'd suspected, Willa stood over the stove and the smell of coffee assaulted her once again sending her tummy into a tailspin.

"Goodness child, sit down," Willa hurried over to her, grabbing Vera's arm as she sunk into a chair. "Are you feeling all right? Should I call for the doctor?"

Taking a deep breath, Vera exhaled slowly. She repeated the process until she felt grounded once again.

"I've been working long hours and haven't been eating as I should." Vera looked at the concerned look at Willa's face. "I'll be fine in a minute."

"Let me get you some coffee," Willa offered, turning back to the stove.

"No!" Vera all but shouted, then said softly, "Just a glass of water or a cup of tea will do the trick."

Willa brought the teapot and a cup to the table, setting it down in front of Vera. "Are you sure I shouldn't get the doctor?"

"I'm fine, really. It will pass soon." Vera poured tea into her cup, then sipped it slowly. The churning in her tummy settled and she felt certain the everyday occurrence had passed.

When she looked up, she found Willa gazing at her with a knowing look in her eye. She felt sick all over again. If Willa figured out she was with child, that meant that others would soon enough as well.

"I'll keep your secret, Vera." Willa smiled, patting Vera's shoulder. "When you are ready then you can tell the world. In the meanwhile, if you need something, anything, you come to me."

"Thank you, Willa," Vera smiled, pushing over the basket of linens. "Do you have anything to go over to Nana's this morning?"

"No, but I will in the morning. I've got a room to prepare today for an arrival." Willa picked up the basket setting it on the kitchen counter.

"Then I'll see you in the morning," Vera said, smiling as she walked out the kitchen door.

"Vera!" Willa called out from the porch of the boardinghouse as Vera rounded the corner. "You forgot your basket."

"Oh goodness, thank you, Willa," Vera said, her cheeks blushing. Taking the basket in her arms she turned back toward Nana's Laundry.

"That girl is going to need someone to look after her and the baby," Willa whispered watching Vera as she waddled slightly across the street. "The question is who?"

"Excuse me, ma'am," a man sat on a coal black horse in front of Willa. "Could you tell me where the livery is?"

Willa accessed the young man with shoulder length blonde hair and piercing blue eyes peeking out from under the well-worn hat. He looked a bit weary and his face was smudged with trail dust. "The livery is down the street and then to your right," she said pointing down the street.

"Thank you, ma'am," the man tipped his hat

then rode away.

Willa watched for a moment then walked back into her boardinghouse. She had a room to prepare for a guest. Other than his name, she only knew that he'd be arriving but not when or for how long. She normally didn't take reservations, but since this request came via telegram she'd hold the room until she needed it. Right now, that wasn't the case since she had plenty of rooms available.

Grabbing the clean linens, Willa went up the steps to the front room. Stepping aside, she quickly looked it over then pulled the sheets off the feather bed to replace them with the fresh ones. Finished, she swept over the top of a dresser and dressing table with a feather duster.

Satisfied the room was now presentable, Willa went back downstairs to find a young man in her parlor. On the floor next to him were a saddle bag and a small satchel.

"Can I help you?" she asked. She immediately recognized him as the stranger who'd asked for directions to the livery.

"I hope so," he said smiling, his dusty hat in his hand. "I'm looking for the proprietor of this boardinghouse."

"And you are?" Willa asked, tempted to take a few steps toward the door in case she needed to run. In a mining town, one never knew what unsavory men wandered in and out. But there was something in this young man's blue eyes that made her feel at ease. And the sense of familiarity scratched in the back of her mind.

"Jack Daniels," Jack announced. "I believe I

have a reservation."

Wallace Baldwin waited as the woman decided if she trusted him or not. He'd seen that look many times, especially when he arrived looking like a saddle tramp. And today he not only looked like one but smelled like he hadn't bathed in weeks.

"Yes, I have a room ready for you Mr. Daniels. I'm Willa Alexander," Willa informed offering her hand. "I'm the owner of the boardinghouse."

Wallace Baldwin wrapped his hand around hers, surprised by the firmness of the older woman's grip. "Nice to meet you, Mrs. Alexander. Please call me Jack."

"I've been wondering when you'd arrive, Jack. Everyone calls me Willa, you may do the same." Willa smiled, then turned back to the stairs she'd just come down. "If you'll follow me, I'll take you to your room. Once you are settled, come back down for a late breakfast. You must be hungry."

"Thank you, Willa," Wallace said, following her up the stairs and to his room.

"Your timing is great, I just put fresh sheets on the bed, so you should be comfortable enough," she said. "There's fresh water in the pitcher for you to clean up with. From the looks of it, I'd say half of Oklahoma red dirt is on you."

"You may be right," Wallace laughed liking Willa almost immediately. "Thank you, Willa."

"Come on down when you're ready and put some food into that gut of yours," Willa said.

Hearing the door click shut, Wallace glanced around the room, then stood looking out the window. It had a perfect view of the street. He'd be able to watch the comings and goings of Blessings Valley without being detected.

When word had reached him that his older brother Thomas had died in a mining accident, his heart wept for all that they'd missed. He'd asked his superiors to be assigned to the investigation and been granted his request under the condition that he kept his personal feelings out of it. He agreed to arrive under the guise of Jack Daniels, to keep his mind on the mining accident, and then to return to Chicago with his report.

Nothing more. Nothing less.

As far as he knew, his brother didn't have a family; at least none he claimed. That fact alone made this assignment much easier. The investigation would be less messy without his brother's widow to contend with.

Unpacking his satchel, he undressed piling the trail dirty clothes on the floor. Once he freshened up a bit, Wallace put on a pair of clean pants, socks, and shirt. Slipping back into the dusty boots, he ran a comb through his damp hair.

"Let's do this and get it over with," he said, heading out of his room with his dirty laundry under his arm.

CHAPTER 2

Willa puttered in the kitchen patiently waiting for her newest boarder, one Jack Daniels, to come down for a late breakfast. And who in their right minds would name a boy after whiskey? A drunkard no doubt.

And why did he look familiar to her? Was it his eyes or something about his face? There'd been many drifters over the years who stayed at her establishment, could he have been with one of them? Or did he remind her of someone she knew in Blessings Valley? If so, who?

Before she could come up with any possibilities, the clop-clop of boots sounded on the floorboards above. Picking up the tray, she walked into the dining room just as Jack Daniels reached the bottom step.

"I trust you are pleased with your room?" she asked, eyeing the bundle of clothes under his arm as she placed the tray on the table.

"Yes, I should be quite comfortable," Jack answered, looking around the room. "Is there a place I can put these to have them cleaned?"

Willa raised her eyebrows. Surely he didn't expect her to wash his dirty laundry. "There's a laundry across the street. You can take them there once you've eaten. In the meantime, just lay them in a chair next to you."

Jack nodded taking a seat next to the chair where he'd dropped his soiled clothing.

"So what brings you to Blessings Valley?" Willa asked taking the plate of eggs, bacon, and biscuits and gravy from the tray, and placing them in front of Jack.

"I'm here to investigate the mining accident for one of the families," Jack answered digging into the food as if he hadn't eaten for a month. "I don't plan on being here very long though. Once I inspect the mine and talk to a few of the miners, I'll be on my way."

"You think you'll find out what caused it after all these months?" Willa asked doubtful there was any evidence left to investigate. The mine had reopened less than a month after the explosion, any evidence of foul play was long gone. "I thought it had been determined to be gas that caused the explosion."

"The family I'm working for isn't satisfied with that explanation." Jack shoveled another fork full of food into his mouth followed by a swig of coffee. "And they would like their son's belongings returned to them. Provided, of course, that I can find them."

"Slow down. I don't want you chocking to death at my table," Willa exclaimed, fighting the urge to remove the plates from in front of him. Instead, she tried to remember if any of the deceased had been single. She came up empty-handed in her memory of even one. So chances were one of the widows was going to feel the pain all over again, and there was nothing she could do to stop it.

"Sorry if I've forgotten my manners. It has been some time since I had a good home cooked meal." Jack said, wiping his mouth with a napkin. "Do you provide meals all day?"

"Thank you and no, I don't. Breakfast is at eight and dinner at seven," Willa answered. She was starting to like this young man. There was something about him that made her believe he was a good, God-fearing man. A man that would be good for Vera. Now if he'd only be around long enough for her to make sure they spent some time together.

"On occasion, I may prepare lunch, but not very often. Otherwise, I'd suggest Millie's Café. The restaurant at the Grand may be a bit more than you'd want to spend. The food at both are equally as good," she said. "The decision is up to you."

"Good to know, thank you for the advice," Jack said, folding his napkin onto his plate.

"Jack, I know how investigations go," Willa said, standing to gather the dishes. "Are you at liberty to say which family you are working for?"

"I don't see any harm," Jack answered, collecting his clothes to be laundered. "Baldwin."

"Thomas Baldwin?" Willa asked, surprised Vera hadn't said anything. Did she even know?

"Yes, Thomas Baldwin," Jack confirmed as he walked toward the door. "Since he didn't have family here, I suspect it will be a quick and easy investigation."

Stunned, Willa watched Jack walk out the door. As he crossed the street toward Nana's Laundry, she knew who he reminded her of.

Vera's late husband Thomas.

Wally strolled across the main street of Blessings Valley assessing the town. A dry goods store. One bank. A saloon. A hotel that looked too rich for even him to stay in it.

There was a newspaper office he'd noticed on his way back from the livery earlier this morning. It was top of his list of where to start asking questions after he deposited his dirty clothes at the laundry.

With any luck, he'd be able to get a small picture of the life his brother led after leaving the family behind. Two years felt like just yesterday, yet it felt like forever since Wally had watched his mother cry as Thomas ride away and never looked back.

Shaking the image away, he stepped through the open door of the laundry. It was as hot and humid inside as it was outside. When the young lady at the counter turned around his heart flipped upside down. She was beautiful. Dark brown hair. Green eyes flecked with gold. The smile on her face that made him think he'd gone to Heaven, didn't match the sadness in her eyes.

"Can I help you?" she asked, placing an empty basket on the counter.

"Um, yea, I have a few things that need to be washed," Wally stammered nearly dropping his bundle on the floor.

"You can put them in here," she said pushing the basket toward him. "You're not from Blessings Valley, are you?"

"No, I'm here on..." Wally began then deciding the fewer people knew why he was in town the more forthcoming they may be with information. "I'm just passing through."

"I saw you this morning riding up to Willa's," she said, writing out a ticket as she inspected his clothes.

"You are quite observant," Wally said, offering his hand to her. "I'm Jack Daniels, but everyone just calls me, Jack. Or whiskey," he laughed.

"I can't understand why," she said sarcastically, her gaze assessing him closely. "These aren't heavily soiled, I'll do my best to see if we can get your things back to you tonight. I must pick up a few things from the boardinghouse before going home. If they are done, I'll bring them with me. You can pay for everything then. Do you want them pressed as well?"

"Thank you," Wally nodded wishing he would be staying around long enough to find out more about her. She may have some valuable information about his brother. "Have a good day."

"You also, Mr. Daniels," the young lady said, the gold flecks in her eyes sparkled briefly with suspicion.

Wally walked out the door then jogged across the street and up the steps of the *Blessings Valley Chronicle*.

"I'll be with you in a moment," the man bent over the printing press called out at the jingle of the bell above the door.

"Of course," Wally answered walking around the newspaper office. One by one he strolled pass copies of the paper on the wall. Each was a copy of that edition's biggest headlines. From tornadoes to the hotel he'd seen.

Then there it was. The front page regarding the mining accident. And another about the findings of the investigation.

Wally's blood ran cold as he read the short articles and looked at the picture of the closed mine opening. Not much information was given; there was nothing about an investigation after the explosion.

His brother had died in the explosion. What Wally read wasn't enough. He wanted answers to take back home to their parents. To let them know where their estranged son is buried and what kind of a life he had led.

"That mining accident is a tragedy many of us are still reeling from," the man's voice came from behind Wally. "The only blessing is that more men weren't killed."

Turning around, Wally roped in his emotions. "What happened?"

"A gas leak, that's what the inspector said. Not that is has helped the widows who stayed behind," the man said shaking his head. "The crew was coming out for lunch when it happened.

Wally's stomach churned at the thought of those wives staying behind. Didn't they have family to care for them?

"It must have been hard for them to go back to their families without their husbands," Wally mused approaching the man. "You said a few stayed behind? How many?"

The man looked at him suspicion darkening his eyes. "If you don't mind me askin', what business is it of yours?"

"I've been hired by one of the families to find out what happened," Wally extended a hand in greeting. "My name is Jack Daniels."

"Humph! Was your father a drunkard to name you after whiskey?" the man smiled slightly, grasping Wally's extended offering. "Clint Wagner and I will tell you straight up. Blessings Valley is protective of the widows who still live here," Clint warned, looking Wally over a bit closer. "Have you been in town before? You look familiar."

"A lot of people have told me that over the years. Guess I have one of those faces," Wally answered attempting to keep from falling down the rabbit hole of Clint Wagner's suspicions.

"Humph, be careful what and who you ask about the mining accident or the widows," Clint warned. "Or you may find yourself buried next to the miners."

"I'll heed your warning. Thank you, Clint," Wally nodded then walked out the door. Standing on the top step, he looked up and down the street deciding where to go next.

"I'll be heading home now, Millie," Vera called out, placing a ticket on top of the freshly pressed clothes in a basket labeled *J Daniels*.

Mollie came out from the back, wiping soap suds from her red hands. "Will you drop off the basket for Mr. Daniels at Willa's then?"

"Yes, and I'll pick up Willa's linens in the morning if that is all right," Vera asked placing a hand on her lower back and stretching the stiffness out. "As well as Mr. Daniel's payment."

"You need to slow down, Vera," Mollie said concern on her face. "I worry about you this early in—"

"Mollie, there is nothing to worry about with me. I am fine," Vera protested knowing she should confirm Millie's suspicions about her pregnancy.

So many times Vera had wanted to tell the

kindly woman it was none of her concern. She was a grown woman and could take care of herself. Even if deep inside, Vera wondered if she'd be able to care for her baby. Thomas's baby.

With no family now other than the good people of Blessings Valley. Thomas never spoke of any so she presumed he had none.

As for her own family, there were enough mouths to feed without adding two more onto her parents' burden. Vera would survive and make a home for herself and her little one.

"Go on home then. I'll see you in the morning," Mollie shook her head giving up on the lecture Vera thought would be coming. Mollie was a kindly woman and Vera liked her very much. "Stop at Willa's on the way here in the morning."

"Thank you, Mollie," Vera smiled relieved that she'd be going home and getting off her feet for the rest of the day.

Coming Soon

ABOUT THE AUTHOR

Maxine Douglas first began writing in the early 1970s while in high school. She took every creative writing course offered at the time and focused her energy for many years after that on poetry. It wasn't until a dear friend's sister revealed she was about to become a published author that jumpstarted Maxine into getting the ball rolling; she finished her first manuscript in a month's time.

Maxine Douglas and her late husband moved to Oklahoma in 2010 from Wisconsin. Since then Maxine has rekindled her childhood love of westerns. She has four children, two granddaughters, and a German Shorthair Pointer named Missy. And many friends she now considers her Oklahoma family.

One of the things Maxine has learned over the years is that you can never stop dreaming and reaching for the stars. Sooner or later you touch one and it'll bring you more happiness than you can ever imagine. Maxine feels lucky, and blessed, that over the past several years she's been able to reach out and touch the stars--and she's still reaching.

Maxine loves to hear from her readers. So, come on by and say "Hello"; Maxine would love to hear from you.

You can catch her on:

Facebook Reader Group:
https://www.facebook.com/groups/maxinesbookdivas/
Twitter: https://twitter.com/wamaxinedouglas
Blog:
http://maxinedouglasauthor.blogspot.com/
Goodreads:
https://www.goodreads.com/author/show/6423715.Maxine_Douglas
BookBub:
https://www.bookbub.com/authors/maxine-douglas

52503645R00163

Made in the USA
Lexington, KY
16 September 2019